*A Promise*
*is a Promise*

# *A Promise is a Promise*

*MOLLY CONE*

*Illustrated by John Gretzer*

1964

HOUGHTON MIFFLIN COMPANY

The Riverside Press Cambridge

also by Molly Cone

THE TROUBLE WITH TOBY
REENEY
THE REAL DREAM
ONLY JANE
TOO MANY GIRLS
MISHMASH
MISHMASH AND THE SUBSTITUTE TEACHER


LIBRARY OF CONGRESS CATALOG CARD NUMBER: 64-20536
PRINTED IN THE U.S.A.

*A Promise*
*is a Promise*

# I



HER brother, Herbert, was going to be thirteen. That's all Ruthy Morgen heard around the house lately was Herbert getting ready to be thirteen. Her grandmother had been baking cookies, her mother had been washing curtains, and her father had been listening to Herbert practicing his speech. Ruthy made a face as she opened the front door.

She stamped through the front hall and into the kitchen. The kitchen floor was covered with newspapers. Her grandmother always covered the kitchen floor with newspapers after it had been washed clean. That's the way Ruthy found it when she came home from school every Friday afternoon. The smell of cleaned floors and windows, and of something baking in the oven usually served to cheer her, whatever her day had been. But not today.

Ruthy's feet ruffled up the newspapers under them, and her grandmother came toward her in a hurry.

"The feet!" said her grandmother, and sighed as she looked at Ruthy's feet.

Ruthy glowered. Both her grandmother and her mother usually sighed whenever they happened to look at Ruthy's feet. Although Ruthy was a year younger than Herbert, her feet were bigger. They weren't even distinctively big, like Sandra Wright's. Sandra had once borrowed her mother's evening shoes and had worn them to school all day. It was doing that sort of thing and not caring what people thought that made Sandra distinctive, Ruthy felt. It was Ruthy's opinion that neither her house nor the family in it had any distinction. Ruthy picked up first one foot and then the other, easing them over the wrinkled paper underneath.

Her grandmother opened the oven door, extracted a hot roll with a quick movement so as not to burn her fingers, and dropped it onto a paper napkin. She put it on the table for Ruthy.

"A taste," she said, her voice dropping to a whisper as if someone might rush in and snatch the roll right out of her hand if she wasn't careful.

Ruthy regarded it, trying not to want it. Made especially for Herbert's party, it looked like a tiny loaf of bread, all braids and twists and full of raisins. She took a bite, expecting it to taste like a bitter pill to her, but surprisingly it tasted very good. She ate it fast, before Herbert should come in. It tasted even better when she thought of Herbert coming in, maybe, and seeing her eating the things being prepared for his party.

Suddenly Ruthy felt a twinge. But she knew it had nothing to do with the morsel she had so hastily swallowed. It was more of an echo of the argument she had

had with Sandra on the way home from school.

"It's his Bar Mitzvah," Ruthy had explained carefully to Sandra.

"You mean your brother has a party as big as a wedding just because he's thirteen!"

It sounded kind of silly the way Sandra said it.

"It's because we're Jewish," Ruthy said, and she did not like the sound of the word in her mouth. There was something about saying *Jewish* — no crisp consonants to clip off, nothing to roll out from the back of your throat.

"I thought you said a Bar Mitzvah was a boy's thirteenth birthday," Sandra said suddenly. She looked at her suspiciously. "Your brother Herbert is almost thirteen and a half. His birthday was last July."

"You have to have a Rabbi for a Bar Mitzvah," Ruthy explained patiently. "Our congregation didn't have a Rabbi last July. The Bar Mitzvah had to wait until the new Rabbi came. That's how come Herbert's Bar Mitzvah will be in November instead of being last July."

Sandra looked a little impressed.

"Everyone in our whole congregation is invited," Ruthy said.

Sandra sniffed. "Our Sunday school teacher is giving a party for us next Saturday," she said. "We can invite anyone we want."

Ruthy had looked at her reflectively.

"Everyone is supposed to come in costume," Sandra said. "Practically everyone in the whole neighborhood is going to be invited."

"Costumes?" It occurred to Ruth that she could wear her queen costume which she had worn as Esther at the Purim festival.

Sandra nodded. "And masks. Everyone is supposed to wear a mask."

Ruthy smiled. She would put Herbert's airplane glue on a white mask and sprinkle sequins over it. They reached the corner where Sandra turned off. They paused, together.

"But I'm not inviting you," Sandra said calmly.

Ruthy felt a lurch of surprise.

"I'm not inviting you because we're only supposed to invite prospective members for our Sunday school class. And I can't invite you because" — she had turned to go down her block and had spoken the last word softly over her shoulder — "as you say — you're Jewish!"

Ruthy pressed her finger down on a crumb remaining on the table, and lifted it to her tongue. Suddenly she wasn't at all sure she cared to be Jewish. Reflectively she rubbed her nose.

The only really Jewish thing about her, she decided, was her nose. She placed her forefinger underneath the tip of her nose, pushing it up. Like her father's, her nose rounded down at the end. Sandra's nose flared elegantly. Marguerite, who lived next door to Sandra, had a nose which turned up. Ruthy pressed harder against the under tip, wondering whether with encouragement it would grow that way.

Her grandmother shifted two pots on the stove, took the lid off one kettle, sniffed at its contents, and turned the burner down below it. She hurried to the cupboard, took out a round box of salt, poured some into the palm of her hand and threw it into the pot. "Herbert likes matzo balls in his soup," she said with satisfaction, and padded back to the cupboard to replace the box of salt.

Ruthy opened the back door and slammed it behind her. *Herbert!* Prince, the dog Herbert had named, raised his head to look lazily at her from his favorite position on the top step.

He was too fat, Ruthy thought, looking at him. His tail was too long, and his legs too short. Her grandmother fed him too much. Things like matzo balls, and scraps of fish, and leftovers from Herbert's plate. He was supposed to be Herbert's dog, but it was their grandmother who fed him. "Hoont," she called him. He even thought that was his name. Ruthy whistled at him sharply.

"Come on, Hoont," she said, disdaining to use the unsuitable name Herbert had given him. The dog ambled after her, down the steps, into the backyard.

She jogged in a circle around the backyard, the dog tagging after. If it wasn't for her, he'd never get any exercise at all, she thought, feeling annoyed with everybody. She picked up her feet the way the boys on the track team did, and circled again.

"That's a dawg," she said encouragingly, holding her head high and bending her knees sharply.

Prince barked and she looked behind with a smile. But the dog was not at her heels. He sat in the middle of the yard, comfortably squatting. He raised only his tail, wagging it, obviously thinking that she was running round like crazy merely to entertain him.

Ruthy stopped. She walked slowly over to the cherry tree. Pulling herself up into it, she sat there thinking about the Sunday school party everyone would be going to. She stared through the branches, over the back fence, to the little house built there, its front door opening onto the alley.

The window shade flickered slightly, and she leaned forward, peering intently. As far back as she could remember, the window shades had always been down on the windows of Mr. Harvey's house. He lived alone. He did his own cooking. He never borrowed anything from the neighbors and he never visited anyone as far as Ruthy knew. Mrs. Byrd, who lived next door to him, didn't like him. She didn't like the tangle of blackberry bushes that grew on his fence and separated his property from hers. She didn't like his two old cats who climbed on her rooftop at night and yowled in cat voices. She felt that his little house, with its flaking paint and overgrown yard, affected the "tone" of the neighborhood.

The door of the little house on the alley opened. Ruthy made her voice very low. "Hi, Mr. Harvey," she called out, and then pulled her head down between her shoulders and hid from sight.

Mr. Harvey looked up to the top of the tree she was in, then up the alley, and down. Then he went back into the house, returned with one big cat which he placed on the doorstep, went back for the other, and closed the door leaving them both outside.

They didn't like being put outside, Ruthy could see. They yowled. One, limping a little, sprang off the porch, took a few steps and went back to the door again. The other jumped to the top of Mrs. Byrd's garbage can in the alley, and toppled the lid off.

Mrs. Byrd's back window opened. She leaned out, her hair in curlers.

"Scat!" she shouted. "You get away from here, you cats!"

Ruthy giggled. Prince, still sitting comfortably in the middle of the yard, raised on four feet, his hair bristling. He barked a short bark.

The cat jumped from the garbage can, ran lightly across the alley and through the left-open gate into Ruthy's yard.

Her mother didn't like the cats in her yard either, Ruthy reflected. She really didn't like them any more than Mrs. Byrd did. "Get 'em!" Ruthy leaned out of the tree to command Prince. The dog bounded forward.

He got behind the cat and yapped at her legs. Ruthy laughed. The cat stood there, its back arched and its tail curled high. But it didn't spit back. It didn't do anything. It just stood there frozen.

Prince ran around and around, making a lot of noise, getting more exercise than he had had in a month. But the cat did not move. A strange feeling crept over Ruthy. She jumped down from the tree at the same moment the door of the little house across the way opened and Mr. Harvey came out waving his cane. With an uneven gait he came hurrying across the alley. Ruthy ran to the dog. "Stop it, Prince!" she shouted. "Stop it!" And though he was in a frenzy, trembling in clumsy excitement, she pulled him away.

The cat shivered. Mr. Harvey scooped her up in his arms and held the cat's face close against his wrinkled neck.

Ruthy put the dog down. "I don't think he really touched her," she said, trying to shake off the guilty feeling.

She followed Mr. Harvey back out of the yard and across the alley. He said not a word to her.

"He's all right, isn't he?" she persisted, standing in the middle of the alley.

Mr. Harvey, with the cat still in his arms, turned at the door to his house. "He's blind in one eye," he said. "Stone-blind. He can't get used to being that way."

"You mean he can't see!" Ruthy's voice raised shrilly.

Mr. Harvey looked at her. "One eye is still pretty good," he said gruffly.

Ruthy turned away, not from Mr. Harvey as much as from the picture in her mind of the cat as she had stood in arched blind fear.

"Wait!" cried Mr. Harvey.

Ruthy stopped, stiffly.

"I want to thank you," he said. He hurried around

the corner of his house, and was back in a moment, in his hands a big yellow rose.

Ruthy held her hands behind her. "You don't have to thank me," she said, eying the yellow flower uncomfortably.

But he pushed the rose toward her. "It is for the kindness in your heart," he said. He made a jerky little bow.

Ruthy felt her face turn red. The rose was in her hand and she could not tell him the truth. She turned and ran across the alley, through her backyard, and into the kitchen. The newspapers ruffled up behind her as she whirled through.

"The feet! The feet!" she heard her grandmother shout after her as she bounded up the stairs, and Herbert's childish tones came to her as she reached the upper hallway. *Baruch, atah, adonoy* . . . He was practicing reading the Hebrew prayers he would have to recite in front of the whole congregation on his Bar Mitzvah. But she gave it no mind. She ran into the bedroom with the rose in her hand and closed the door.

## 2

SHE stood there scowling at it. Downstairs, the doorbell rang. Herbert hollered from his room — "Hey! Someone answer the doorbell!"

Ruthy's shoulders twitched, but she didn't move. She heard Herbert open the door of his room and clatter down the stairs, the sound of the front door opening and closing, then, the slow tread of his footsteps coming up the steps again.

"Hey!" he called out to her. "It's a present — for me!" He kicked at Ruthy's door.

She threw the rose into her open top drawer, and shut it with a bang. "You stay out of here!" she shouted, and she waited for the inevitable reaction. He would probably stealthily turn the handle and thrust the door open wide. But he did nothing of the sort. She waited a moment, listening. Herbert was walking down the hallway to his room, whistling brightly.

They had chicken soup for dinner that night. They always had chicken soup on Friday nights, sometimes with matzo balls. Sandra would call them dumplings, Ruthy guessed, and she frowned at them.

"Oh boy!" said Herbert. "Matzo balls!"

Her grandmother beamed, and her mother and father looked at Herbert with that sickening expression they wore whenever they looked at Herbert lately. As if having lived long enough to be celebrating a Bar Mitzvah was a special accomplishment. Herbert was the only grandson her grandmother had, so Ruthy guessed she could excuse her grandmother's air of worshipful wonder. But that didn't excuse her mother and father. All the Jewish families they knew had celebrated their sons' thirteenth birthday with big Bar Mitzvahs. Some of them even gave receptions at the Athletic Club. Herbert and all the boys in his Sunday school class had been going to midweek classes in the Rabbi's study, studying for their Bar Mitzvahs. There were certain things they had to learn about the religion, and about the prayer books, and, most particularly about the Torah. They had to learn to read from the Torah which was the Bible written in Hebrew letters, just to prove that they could read Hebrew, she guessed. And they had to learn all about the ritual like why candles were lit every Friday night, and why Jewish people weren't supposed to eat ham.

"If you're not going to eat your matzo balls, I'll eat them for you," Herbert offered righteously.

Herbert's face was small and thin. His hair was sand-colored, and his eyelashes were straight and no color at all. He lifted his chin when he talked, usually, as if what he said was terribly important. This time, because his mouth was full, he screwed up his face too. Ruthy glared at him. And although she had not intended to eat the matzo balls, she did. Her mother only looked at her disapprovingly. No one ever patted her on the head for doing anything, she thought bitterly.

Her grandmother was gazing at her. "Too much salt maybe?" she asked anxiously.

Ruthy shook her head. They were all looking at her.

"I've been thinking of joining Sandra's Sunday school class, maybe," she said loudly, listening to the words as they came out. Actually, she had not given it any conscious thought, but now that she had said it, she began to give it some consideration.

Her grandmother's soup spoon clattered to the table. For a moment Ruthy was pleased with their fixed attention. It was the first time they had looked at her, really looked at her, since Herbert had begun to prepare for his Bar Mitzvah.

"A church?" whispered her grandmother, her eyes opening so wide that her brow was furrowed with wrinkles.

Her father laid his soup spoon back into his bowl, put his elbows on the table, crossed his arms and gazed at her.

Her mother stared.

Only Herbert was unperturbed. He went on eating his chicken soup and matzo balls. "It's the party," he pronounced lightly.

Mrs. Morgen exchanged a worried glance with her husband. "What party?"

"Everybody is invited to go to a Sunday school party. There's only one catch. You've got to be thinking of joining the class."

"Well, I'm thinking," said Ruthy. "I've been thinking about it a lot lately. It seems kind of silly for me to be going all the way across town to the Beth El Congregation when there's a perfectly good Sunday school right here in the neighborhood."

Her father took his elbows off the table, and pulled off a small chunk of bread from the twisted loaf before him. "There's no law against thinking," he said calmly, and went on eating as if that ended the matter.

Ruthy remembered the time when she was eight or nine years old and had packed her bag and announced that she was leaving home. She remembered that her father had only opened the front door wide, and had pointed with his arm extended, and had said — "Go!"

She had gone — around the house and back in through the kitchen door, where her grandmother had let her in, pretending not to see her.

Thoughtfully she looked at her father. He looked like a little boy going bald. There was a bare spot right across the top of his head. There was a crevice in his chin, and a spot of soup below that. Because it was Friday night, he wore a tie, and his coat buttoned, rather snugly, over his middle. Her father was getting fat, Ruthy reflected. And she was no longer eight or nine years old.

She looked at the roast chicken sitting on the platter before her father. He stood up to carve it. Sandra's family always had ham on Sunday, Ruthy knew. She had never in all her life tasted a piece of ham, Ruthy reflected, and ate her chicken, pretending it was ham.

"Tastes just like chicken," she said to herself, but aloud, and smiled at her private joke as her mother looked at her, regarding the well-gnawed drumstick on her plate. Ruthy did not bother to explain.

Her grandmother began to tell Mr. Morgen who had been sent invitations to the Bar Mitzvah. "Mrs. Kittlemeyer and her two daughters who came from Germany," she said counting off on her fingers, "and the cousin to Mrs. Kaplan who is the new professor at the college. And Mr. Svenson."

"Mr. Svenson?" Mr. Morgen asked. You could see he had never heard of Mr. Svenson.

"Of course, Mr. Svenson," her grandmother said, shaking her head at being interrupted in her listing.

Ruthy's mother explained—"He owns the fish market on the waterfront and always saves the best white salmon for us."

Mr. Morgen nodded agreeably.

"I never knew Mr. Svenson was Jewish," Ruthy remarked.

Her grandmother looked at her severely. "Did I say he was Jewish?"

"But you're inviting him to the Bar Mitzvah."

"There's no law that says that everybody invited to a Bar Mitzvah has to be Jewish," her grandmother said. "To have a Bar Mitzvah, you are Jewish, yes, but not to go and sit and listen and congratulate."

"I invited my gym teacher, Mr. Jones," Herbert spoke up.

The severe glance was transferred to Herbert. "And why only your gym teacher? Why not your Latin teacher?"

Ruthy grinned. Her grandmother had never understood how Herbert, a Jewish boy, could have such admiration for a teacher who did not teach from books. She had said often enough, "You send a boy to school to study and learn, not to climb ropes like monkeys." To her athletics was no different than fighting. If you had to get something by fighting with your fists, then you deserved the bloody noses. There were other ways, she felt, that were better ways to achieve the same ends. "Jewish boys shouldn't fight," she had told Herbert over and over again. "If you fight in your home, you'll fight at school, and if you fight at school you'll fight in the street, and if you fight in the street, pretty soon one neighborhood will be fighting against another neighborhood, and one city against another, and one country against another country." At this point, she usually threw up her hands in despair.

Ruthy's grandmother had a simple solution to abolish wars. It was — everyone should stop all the fighting.

"If you're inviting Mr. Svenson, and Herbert is inviting Mr. Jones, why can't I invite Sandra?" Ruthy asked.

Her mother turned to her with a look of surprise. "Did I ever say you couldn't invite Sandra?"

"I guess I never asked," Ruthy admitted. She thought of Sandra having a Sunday school party and not inviting her. "To tell you the truth," she said, "I'm not sure I even want to invite Sandra."

Herbert grinned at her. "Be sure to tell her she doesn't have to become Jewish to come to my Bar Mitzvah," he advised.

Ruthy ignored him. But she had no intention of inviting Sandra to Herbert's Bar Mitzvah if Sandra did not invite her to the Sunday school party.

"Are you inviting Eddie?" Herbert interrupted his grandmother as she continued to recite names and identifying characteristics of those on the guest list.

"What reminded you of Eddie?" Mrs. Morgen said.

Herbert shrugged. "Oh, I just thought maybe we should invite him to the Bar Mitzvah."

Mrs. Morgen pressed her lips together. His grandmother snorted. "A no-good like that!" she said.

Ruthy sat up straight and began to listen carefully. She had often heard stories about their cousin Eddie. She had gone to his Bar Mitzvah when she was five years old, and had spilled pink punch all down the front of her dress. She remembered Eddie because of the dress. For a time her mother and grandmother had talked about him only in whispers. He had been too smart for his own good was the way her grandmother had put it. He was always in trouble.

"The kids were talking about him in the Rabbi's class today," Herbert said. "Someone said he's thinking about turning Catholic."

Mrs. Morgen put in quickly, "And where was the Rabbi while you boys were wasting time making up stories about Eddie?"

Herbert grinned. "He was there," he said. "He was the one who told us."

Mr. and Mrs. Morgen's glances met across the table. They hadn't made up their mind yet about the Rabbi. He was new and had only lately come to their congregation. As far back as Ruthy could remember, the congregation to which they belonged had changed Rabbis "every Monday and Thursday," as her grandmother put it. It was a conservative congregation. But some people were more conservative than others, Ruthy guessed. The last Rabbi had been "a little too orthodox" for some people's tastes, and this new Rabbi, Ruthy could see already, was going to be "too reform."

Every Jewish congregation was either orthodox, conservative or reform. Those who were orthodox, to Ruthy's way of thinking, were the Jews who never took off their little black skullcaps, and prayed every day and out loud, and never ate ham. And those who were reform were Jewish people who didn't believe in wearing hats to pray in, and sometimes didn't even believe in some of the old customs. To be conservative was to be right in the middle. Wearing hats but not all the time. Keeping the old customs, but changing them a little. Ruthy had a feeling that if their grandmother had not been living with them, her own parents would have preferred to be reform. As far as she could see, there wasn't any real difference. They were still all Jewish.

Suddenly she wondered whether Eddie was really as crazy as everyone thought he was.

Mr. Morgen cleared his throat. "I hope you're well prepared for your Bar Mitzvah," he said. "It's in two weeks, you know."

"I know, I know," said Herbert, but he was watching Ruthy with a funny look.

Her grandmother went on with the listing of the guests, but Ruthy didn't bother to listen any more. For something had occurred to her. Something so simple that she wondered she hadn't thought of it before.

She looked around the table thinking how easy it would be, and touched her nose absently. After all she would be wearing a mask, wouldn't she?

# 3

RUTHY slipped out the back way, crossed the yard, and ducked into the alley. Mr. Harvey's shades were down, as usual, she noted in passing. But the window shade quivered as she went past, and she saw that it was pulled aside a little. Mr. Harvey's round face nodded and smiled at her before it fell back into place again. She pretended not to notice as she hurried on.

Sandra was sitting on her back porch, restringing her pearl beads. "I'm going to wear them to the party," she said.

"The party," said Ruthy, sitting down on the step beside Sandra. She primly brought her knees together.

Sandra regarded her solemnly. "It isn't that I don't want to invite you," she said importantly. "It's just that we aren't supposed to invite anybody but — well you know."

"But people who are interested," Ruthy supplied promptly. She knew exactly what she was going to say. But she leaned back and stared at the darkening shadows in the alley, wanting to say it exactly right. "To tell you the truth, I've never given much thought to joining your Sunday school class — " she paused delicately and picked up a pearl — "before."

Sandra dropped her beads into her lap. "You mean, you would!"

Ruthy replied carefully. "Well, I'm not really sure that I would, but I've certainly thought about it."

Sandra looked at her suspiciously. "You really are thinking about joining our Sunday school class?"

"That's what I told my father," Ruthy said truthfully.

"You mean you told your father!"

"Of course he didn't exactly approve of the idea," Ruthy said.

"Well you don't have to decide anything yet," Sandra said quickly. "Not everybody who will be going to the party will actually join. It's just supposed to be an encouragement — to those who are thinking about it. So you're invited."

Ruthy congratulated herself. She had figured exactly right. You didn't have to sign on the dotted line or anything. You just had to think about it.

"My mother said that if you're once a Jew, you're always a Jew. That's what *she* said," Sandra put her beads down to stare curiously at Ruthy.

It occurred to Ruthy that Mrs. Wright had always been scrupulously polite to Mrs. Morgen when they met at the supermarket or P.T.A. meeting, or anywhere. Not unfriendly, but not exactly friendly either. "I have a cousin who's turned Catholic," Ruthy said, offhandedly.

Sandra digested this. "Well, I guess it's all right

then." She giggled. "I thought maybe being Jewish was something you were born with, like a hunchback or something, that you couldn't ever change. I never thought of it as just a religion like everybody has."

Ruthy straightened her shoulders, sitting stiffly on the porch steps. She didn't say anything for a little while. Sandra went right on talking.

"I'm going to wear a tutu," Sandra said, preening a little. "Marguerite Jensen lent it to me. It's pink with sequins." She added, "Marguerite can't go. She has to go to a piano recital."

"That's nice of her," Ruthy said with an edge of politeness.

Slyly Sandra said, "You mean nice to lend me her tutu, or nice that she has to go to a piano recital."

Ruthy glanced quickly to the house next door where Marguerite lived, then she and Sandra looked at each other and laughed together.

"My queen costume has five yards on the skirt," Ruthy said, feeling a satisfaction. "Three petticoats. There's a tiara that goes with it, all sparkly, like diamonds."

Sandra looked at her respectfully. "We can go together," Sandra said. "You can bring your costume over to my house and we can change and go together. Maybe my mother will drive us there."

Ruthy smiled. It was even easier than she had thought it would be.

Suddenly Sandra leaned toward her. She glanced quickly over her shoulder, and put her finger to her lips. "Remember mum's the word," she said.

The significance was not lost on Ruthy. She, Ruthy Morgen, would pretend she was not Jewish and a candidate for membership in the Community Church Sunday school class. Ruthy felt a strange uncertain beating in her chest. But she nodded.

"Mum's the word," she said firmly.

# 4

RUTHY heard Mrs. Byrd yelling at Mr. Harvey's cats even before she came down her back porch steps with the Queen Esther costume carefully rolled in a bundle under her coat. It had been fairly easy to leave the house without anyone noticing. Saturday was a quiet day at the Morgens'. Her grandmother never went into the kitchen at all that day. She always did the cooking for the weekend on Friday. On Saturday, she dressed in a silk print dress and went visiting, or merely sat in the living room and "rested." It was the day Mrs. Morgen went shopping downtown.

Neither Ruthy nor Herbert was supposed to "work" on Saturday. They could study or read or play quietly, or go to a show. Mr. Morgen was the only one in the family who worked on Saturday, because in a city as small as Olympus you couldn't very well close your business on a day when most people came to town to shop. But he marked the day also as a day of rest by not unpacking racks of clothing, nor did he do any alterations on Saturday. If a customer bought a pair of trousers on Saturday from Sam Morgen, he had to wait until Monday to have them altered to his measure.

The electric clock on the kitchen wall had seemed to

jerk violently as Ruthy had crept out of the kitchen, and her stomach had lurched with it. Then she had to smile at herself. Her father hadn't said she couldn't go to the party. To be honest about it, she guessed it had never occurred to him that she really would go. But he hadn't said she shouldn't.

She shifted the bundle out from under her coat as soon as she crossed the backyard and entered the alley.

Mr. Harvey's two cats were sitting on the stoop of Mr. Harvey's house washing their faces. Mrs. Byrd was leaning out of her window glaring suspiciously at the cats. Mr. Harvey unperturbably tended to his rosebushes. Mr. Harvey was very proud of his rosebushes. He never cut them, but always pinched off the roses after they had reached full bloom. He had been placing the roseleaves in an old apple box set next to his front step, adding a few every day. The box gave off a pleasantly unpleasant rotting dry-rose smell. As Ruthy walked by, Mr. Harvey raised his garden shears in his cotton-gloved hand to wave at her, and she nodded quickly and hurried on.

Sandra's door opened for Ruthy even before she reached it. Sandra wore Marguerite's pink tutu. Her upper legs were fat and pink too, almost as pink as the delicate shade of the costume. Ruthy blinked at her. The sequins flashed brilliantly as Sandra ran out to greet Ruthy.

"I thought you were never coming!" Sandra said. She moved about on her toe tips as if she were a dancer in a ballet. "I'm all ready. Except for my mask. But we won't put on our masks until we get there."

Ruthy followed Sandra into her bedroom. Sandra's room had a single bed in it. It was covered with stuffed animals. Over her headboard hung a sampler worked in cross-stitch in blue and red. Sandra must have made it herself when she was in the second or third grade. It spelled out "Jesus loves little children." Ruthy averted her eyes and began to change into her costume.

When she had fastened the side zipper, and the snaps at the wrists, and adjusted the five-yard full skirt, she walked into Sandra's living room feeling a little self-conscious.

Mrs. Wright was there dusting the furniture. "You look very nice," she said automatically, and pulled a chair away from the wall to recover a magazine which had slipped behind. Saturday Mrs. Wright always cleaned her house.

"Mother gave us some bus tokens," Sandra said, exhibiting them on the palm of her hand.

Ruthy looked at the small disks. "You mean we're going on the bus?" Her voice rose oddly. It had never occurred to her that they would have to go to the party on the bus. She had supposed that Mrs. Wright would drive them in her car, or in lieu of that, that Sandra would arrange to have someone pick them up. She swallowed. She saw herself going on the bus, the skirt of the queen costume dragging on the bus floor as they went down the aisle, the skirt taking up two seats instead of one.

Mrs. Wright looked at Ruthy a moment, her lips pursed. "Why don't you hoist up the skirt a bit," she suggested. "I'm sure your coat will cover most of it if you hold it up as you walk."

Ruthy looked down at the long, full skirt. She tried wrapping it around her body above her knees, and held it there with one arm as Sandra helped her into her coat. She wished suddenly she had thought of wearing something other than a queen costume, and she looked enviously at Sandra's bare pink legs.

They waited on the street corner, Sandra dancing around in her tutu, which was completely hidden by her coat, Ruthy standing stiff and straight clutching her skirt to keep it from falling down. Luckily the bus came almost at once, but it started off again as soon as they mounted, and Ruthy had to grab the bar above to keep her balance. The skirt hem flopped to her ankles. The people in the bus stared at her curiously. Sandra, who had made her way down the aisle, quickly had found a seat in the back. She motioned Ruthy to sit beside her.

Ruthy looked at Sandra, sitting there with her legs bare and her coat neatly buttoned up, and for a moment hated her. She frowned at Sandra, and shook her head, and stood where she was. She stared out the window the whole time pretending she wasn't noticing everybody noticing her. When the bus stopped at

the proper corner, she hiked up her skirt, and pushed out as fast as she could, leaving the smiles and grins and chuckles behind.

The Sunday school teacher lived on a wide avenue lined with old trees. Most of the leaves had fallen and lay thickly on the sidewalks. The lawns were neatly trimmed in this area, and the shrubbery clipped in a formal manner. The hedges were square; the bushes on either side of the entry round. They mounted the stone steps leading up to the door. It was an old house — "almost fifty years old," Sandra whispered. There was an old-fashioned knocker on the door which resounded with a dull thud as Sandra lifted it and let it drop. And they stood there out on the stone porch a moment or two before anybody inside heard it.

Then there was a scramble on the other side of the door, and a voice said, "Isn't there someone at the door?" And someone else said, "I didn't hear anything." And then the door opened.

Quickly Ruthy adjusted her mask.

"Hello Mrs. Harrington," Sandra shrieked. Mrs. Harrington, whose long thin face was only half covered by her mask, smiled a thin smile and said, "Go right down to the recreation room, girls — everybody is down there," and hurried off in the other direction.

Behind her mask, Ruthy smiled. She followed Sandra down the long winding stairs to the basement recreation room. She stumbled only a little on her long skirt. A boy passed them going up. He was dressed as a cowboy.

"A queen!" he called back over his shoulder to the boy behind him. "And a pink mouse, I think."

"I'm not a mouse!" shrieked Sandra. "I'm a dancer. Don't you recognize a tutu when you see one?"

Both boys laughed. "Who-who?" one said.

"Tutu!" said Sandra.

The boys turned around and walked back down with Sandra, and Ruthy in her big skirt dragged on behind. She wished suddenly she had worn something a little more interesting than a queen costume.

But she forgot about her regret when they reached the bottom of the stairs. Orange and black crepe paper ribbons decorated the low-ceilinged room. In the fireplace was set a black witch's pot. Under it a fire made of orange crepe paper and a flashlight, Ruthy guessed, blazed. The place was full of gypsies and hoboes and spacemen, and witches and goblins. There was one king with a Vote-for-Me emblem on his chest, and a crown of gold. But though she was pleased when he waved to her, she pretended not to notice.

Mrs. Harrington soon came down and started everyone playing games. They played something called "Going to Jerusalem" which Ruthy privately thought was not much different from the old kid game of musical chairs. Then they had a relay race, and after that she carried peanuts across the room on a knife to deposit them in a jar. Ruthy was surprised when they counted the peanuts she had carried and found that she had the most.

"You mean I won!" she cried out in amazement.

"You certainly did," Mrs. Harrington said gaily — "whoever you are!" She peered closely at Ruthy for a moment.

Ruthy held her breath.

"I can't seem to recognize anyone!" Mrs. Harrington gave a little laugh and handed her a prize.

Ruthy turned it over and over.

"Open it!" shouted one of the girls in the group eagerly clustered about her.

The prize was wrapped in orange tissue paper tied with a black ribbon. Pleased to be the center of attention, Ruthy carefully untied the bow and unwound the paper. She looked at the prize in her hand.

"Ohhhhhh," said someone at her right.

"Gee, I wish I had won that," said someone else at her left.

Ruthy wished she had too. For the prize was a cross. It was a small plastic cross on a gold-colored chain. "Thank you," she said politely. But no one really heard her.

She held back on the next game, pretending she was not really interested in playing. The truth was, she didn't want to take a chance on winning any more such prizes. Even holding the little cross in her hand gave her an uncomfortable feeling. She looked about on her skirt, but a queen evidently had no need for pockets. She laid it down on the edge of a chair, and pretended she still had it in her hand when she moved off. But only a few moments went by before a girl rushed up to her dangling the chain from her fingers.

"Here!" she said. "Here's your cross! You almost lost it!"

Ruthy felt it back in the palm of her hand again. "Thank you," she said weakly.

She moved it from one hand to the other, edging around the rim of the group, and she looked around, wondering what she could do with it. At the other end of the room, pushed into an alcove under a high window, she saw a puffy davenport. She moved toward it, cautiously. Its arms were threadbare, and its cushions were knobby and uneven. A sofa like this in her own house would have been long since given to the junkman. Fleetingly, she heard her grandmother's voice — "A shame for the neighbors." She grinned, and feeling the cross in her hand, guiltily put the thought of her grandmother out of her mind.

Ruthy sat down on the broken sofa. She stayed there only a moment pretending to be terribly interested in watching the game going on in the center of the room. But as she watched, she stuck her hand behind the cushion — down into the back — and when she pulled it out again, it was empty.

Ruthy exhaled deeply, jumped up and moved again into the center of the room. It was strange how free she felt.

A tall boy skidded up to her. "Hey! You're Margie, aren't you?"

She smiled back. "Maybe," she said, and she moved quickly on. She guessed the mask covered her face very well.

Sandra danced up to her. "Isn't this a good party!" Sandra looked pink all over, Ruthy reflected. Even her face had turned pink in its excitement. Ruthy thought of the boy calling her Margie, and answered with enthusiasm, "Wonderful!"

But somehow she was not having as good a time as she had expected to have. She was happy to see two women come down the stairs bearing trays of doughnuts. She was one of the first to crowd about when Mrs. Harrington clapped her hands for attention.

"It's about time," Sandra whispered to her. "I'm starved."

"Before we have our refreshments," Mrs. Harrington was making her thin voice as loud as she could, "we will all unmask." She raised her hands to the sides of her mouth. "All those bringing guests will please bring them up to me to be introduced before you help yourself to refreshments!"

Suddenly Ruthy didn't feel very hungry. "C'mon," she said to Sandra, pulling at her arm. "It's awfully late. I think we'd better go home."

But Sandra's eyes were on the doughnuts. With a firm grip on Ruthy's arm, she pulled her forward into the line forming before Mrs. Harrington. "Take off your mask," Sandra ordered, removing her own.

Ruthy pretended there was something wrong with the fastening. Then reluctantly took it off. Maskless, she stood face-to-face with Mrs. Harrington.

"This is my prospective member," Sandra said. "Her name's Ruthy Morgen."

Mrs. Harrington looked surprised. "Ruthy Morgen?" she repeated. She gazed at Ruthy. "Sam Morgen's daughter?"

Ruthy said bravely, quickly, "I haven't exactly made up my mind which Sunday school I want to go to."

Mrs. Harrington smiled. "How nice of you to come," she said kindly, and turned to the next in line.

Sandra giggled as she drew Ruthy on to the refreshment table. Ruthy didn't say anything. She ate the doughnut Sandra proffered her, pushing it into her mouth automatically, and swallowed without tasting anything.

She hardly remembered the ride back on the bus. And when she got to Sandra's house, she pulled the costume off, bundled it up quickly, and ran down the alley toward home. The kitchen was exactly as she had left it only two and one half hours before. She heard voices from the other room. Quickly she opened the door to the basement and went down the stairs.

There was a rummage barrel there next to the washing machine. Ruthy pushed the costume down into it, stirring up the old clothes lying in there to get it to the bottom.

When she came back up the stairs, she was sure about only one thing. She never wanted to see that costume again.

# 5

HER grandmother was bustling about the kitchen when Ruthy came upstairs. The kettle was boiling on the stove; the refrigerator door hung open. Mrs. Morgen transferred several covered bowls and jars from the refrigerator to the kitchen counter. The day of rest was over. Ruthy closed the basement door behind her.

"Ruthy, set the table," her mother said over her shoulder.

Ruthy placed the mats on the kitchen table before taking the plates from the cupboard shelves. On Saturday night they usually ate in the kitchen. It was more supper than dinner, really, for nothing special was planned. On Saturday nights they ate cold cuts and rye bread, and sliced tomatoes maybe, and perhaps some of the coffee cake baked on Friday. Her grandmother took the kettle off the stove and filled the teapot. Mr. Morgen came into the kitchen and opened the refrigerator.

"The herring is on the table," her grandmother said. Mr. Morgen closed the refrigerator door. He sat down at the kitchen table.

"Well, Ruthy," he said.

Ruthy put the salt and pepper shakers on the table.

She didn't say anything.

"Where's Herbert?" her father said.

Her grandmother answered. "Where should he be? He's studying." Ruthy listened to the pride in her voice. "Go call him, Ruthy. Tell him to come to eat."

Obediently Ruthy went to the bottom of the stairs. "Herbert!" she hollered.

The front door opened and Herbert came in.

"I thought you were supposed to be studying," Ruthy said ungraciously.

"I was out waiting for the mailman," he said importantly. "He always comes later on Saturdays." Herbert held up a handful of small envelopes. "They're pouring in!" he said dramatically.

Ruthy sat down at the table and began to butter a slice of bread. Herbert set the bunch of small envelopes down on the middle of the table next to the sliced tomatoes, and took a gulp of milk before sitting down. Her mother poured a cup of tea, and sat down, too. But her grandmother seemed most eager of all. She wiped her hands on her apron, sat down, and gathered all the envelopes into her lap. Mrs. Morgen had ordered the Bar Mitzvah invitations and had affixed the stamps, but it was her grandmother who was keeping count of who were coming and who weren't.

The invitations had been printed on a white card with a tissue paper over the printing. The inner card had its own special envelope. A tiny card and envelope had also been enclosed for the reply. The two envelopes — the one holding the invitation card, and the one holding the reply card — had been put into a larger envelope which had been addressed in her grandmother's hand in blue ink to each guest. It seemed like a lot of unnecessary trouble to Ruthy, for some Bar Mitzvahs were merely announced at Friday night services and everyone in the congregation was invited, and that was that. But invitations had been sent out for Herbert's Bar Mitzvah because their grandmother wanted to make sure everyone was personally invited. After all, Herbert was her only grandson. You'd think, thought Ruthy, that it was *her* Bar Mitzvah instead of Herbert's. She looked at her grandmother.

The elder Mrs. Morgen held one of the small envelopes open in her hands. She was frowning.

"What's the matter?" Mr. Morgen asked.

"Etta Kaplan, she can't come."

Mrs. Morgen put down her cup of tea. "How can that be! I saw her myself only a few days ago. She said she and her mother were looking forward to the Bar Mitzvah. She even offered to make pickled herring for the reception."

"What does she say?" Mr. Morgen asked, forgetting to drink his tea.

The grandmother read aloud: " 'With regrets,' it says, 'I will not be able to attend your son's Bar Mitzvah. Respectfully, Etta Kaplan.' "

"Respectfully?" Mr. Morgen thrust out his lower lip, opening his eyes wide. He shrugged then, took a slice of bread, placed it on his plate, slathered it with mustard and folded it over.

"You forgot the salami." Herbert nudged him.

Mr. Morgen opened his sandwich again, and added several slices of salami. "I was overcome with the picture of Etta's respect," he explained . . . "I've never known Etta to be so respectful — unless she's mad at somebody."

"Nonsense!" said Ruthy's grandmother. "What has she got to be mad about?"

"If you know Etta," Mr. Morgen said, after swallowing a bite of his sandwich, "you know she has a special talent. She can make a lot out of a little."

"Like delicious cookies out of scraps of dough," Mrs. Morgen said absently. She took the reply card and looked at it herself, a small wrinkle appearing between her eyes.

"And mountains out of molehills," Herbert put in brightly.

His grandmother frowned at him.

"I just can't imagine having a Bar Mitzvah without Etta," Mrs. Morgen said. And Ruthy looked at her closely. There was a peculiar note in her voice. Was she glad, Ruthy wondered, or sorry.

Etta Kaplan was one of Mrs. Morgen's cousins. They were the same age though Etta had never married. She lived with her mother, and as Ruthy's father had once put it, they kept themselves busy telling each other what to do and how it should be done. They were both big women and when Ruthy was younger she had never been sure which was the mother and which the daughter. Personally, she couldn't see how knowing which was which would make any difference. She had usually avoided them when she had been younger and they had come to visit, for although they were her mother's cousins, and considered themselves so refined, they talked in loud voices, and always asked how much everything cost, and mingled their praises with just enough surprise to leave you with the feeling that they had never had much of an opinion of you.

"You mean she's not coming to my Bar Mitzvah?" Herbert said. He didn't sound at all unhappy.

Their grandmother, instead of answering, pushed her chair back from the table and stood up.

"Where are you going?" Ruthy's mother called after her.

"To the telephone. Where else should I be going?"

They watched as she opened the desk drawer. "Ruthy," she said, "look up the number for me." She pulled out the telephone book.

Ruthy opened the book to the K's and looked down the column. Her grandmother, the telephone already in her hand, carefully dialed the number Ruthy read out to her.

"Etta?"

Everyone at the kitchen table stopped eating and strained to hear.

"And why are you not coming to my Herbert's Bar Mitzvah? Are you sick?" She listened a moment.

"She's not sick," said Mr. Morgen softly.

"You're not coming because of your mother? Your mother is sick?" She listened again.

"Her mother's not sick," Mr. Morgen mumbled. Mrs. Morgen shook her head at him.

Suddenly the elder Mrs. Morgen shrieked, "Of course I invited your mother!"

"She's not coming because we didn't invite her mother!" Mr. Morgen said triumphantly.

"I wrote the invitations myself!" the elder Mrs. Morgen said emphatically. "Separate? Wait. Let me think. No, not separate. I remember it exactly now. The one invitation. Two names. One invitation." She listened again.

"No!" she said in tone of disbelief. "Oh my!" She turned a moment to the family at the table. "I must have forgotten to write in the second name," she said and went back to the telephone. "Let me talk to Blanche, please, a minute." She waited. "Blanche? Yes, yes. Of course. A mistake. How could it be anything but a mistake!" She waited until the conversation from the other end of the line had come to an end. "I will see you at my Herbert's Bar Mitzvah then?" She smiled. "Fine," and she hung up.

"It was a mistake," she said. She came back to the

table and drank her cup of tea. Then she had to go over it all again, as if they had not been sitting right there the whole time.

Ruthy thought of her family sitting there getting excited about an invitation to a Bar Mitzvah. It was the sort of thing that couldn't happen in Sandra's family. The biggest party Sandra's family had ever had was her brother's wedding. The invitations were *engraved.* And there weren't very many of them. Ruthy had been invited as Sandra's friend, and to her mind the church had been half empty. The groom's friends and relatives sat on one side of the church and the bride's family and friends on the other side. Not all mixed up as Jewish weddings were. And after the ceremony, all they served were little tiny sandwiches on white bread with the crusts cut off, and small squares of cake. You had your choice of coffee or punch. That's all.

The bride, as she had looked dressed in a full white gown with a train, came to Ruthy's mind. For no reason, she thought of the queen costume hidden in the barrel. Quickly Ruthy drank her milk.

"Who's going to help me practice my speech?" Herbert asked loudly, importantly.

Mrs. Morgen said, "You mean you don't know your speech and it's only one week before your Bar Mitzvah!"

"I know it fine," Herbert said. "I just don't want to forget it."

"You'll know it; you'll know it," the grandmother said with conviction.

"Okay, I'll help you," Ruthy said wearily, but she offered only because what she didn't want to do was to think about what had happened that day.

# 6

Ruthy listened to Herbert recite the prayers he would say as he stood before the congregation on Saturday morning at his Bar Mitzvah. It gave her a righteous feeling to be helping him, and she rather enjoyed it.

"Say your words more distinctly," she said, taking pains to speak distinctly herself.

Herbert started over.

"Louder," she said, enjoying to the fullest her position of aid. She listened carefully, calling his attention to his mispronunciation of a word, his improper emphasis of a syllable in a word, and the insufficient pause he made at the end of a sentence.

She stopped him again and again. "Now repeat," she said, frowning at him.

But he only frowned back at her.

"What's the matter?" she asked impatiently.

"You don't know how I'm supposed to do it!"

Ruthy thought of all the times she had heard these words recited. She sniffed. "I could say it blindfolded," she told him. "I've heard it so often, I could give your speech and read your prayers, and do it better than you can, I bet!"

Herbert hooted. "It doesn't make any difference

how well you can read my Bar Mitzvah part," he pointed out. "You could do it better than anybody in the whole world and it still wouldn't be any good when you did it! Because Bar Mitzvah is only for boys. A girl can't have a Bar Mitzvah."

Ruthy only glared at him.

Their grandmother came out of the kitchen. "Some congregations have Bar Mitzvahs for girls," she remarked. "Only they call it *Bas* Mitzvah. Bar for boys and Bas or Bat for girls. We've never celebrated Bas Mitzvahs in our congregation. But that doesn't mean it hasn't been in a lot of places." She looked at Herbert severely and went back into the kitchen.

The mailbox clanged open and shut and Ruthy rushed to the front door almost as eagerly as Herbert.

"Anything for me?" Herbert said automatically, before she had even taken the mail from the box.

She made a face. "It's all for you," she said, handing it over.

Herbert tore open a large-size envelope. Out of it he drew a white card. There was an embossed design on it. He studied it carefully.

"Hey! I guess I own some trees in Israel," he said.

Ruthy examined the certificate carefully. As she read the small print, she snorted. "You don't own them," she said with disparagement. "It's just a donation. The money goes to Israel to buy trees to be planted there, and this card goes to you. That's all you get — the certificate."

"It's the same thing," Herbert said. "Some day I'll be in Israel and I'll see some trees and I'll know how they got there."

"So?" Ruthy wondered what was so great about that. She handed back the certificate.

For a moment he stared at it thoughtfully. "I wonder what it would feel like to live in Israel."

Ruthy shrugged. "I guess it wouldn't feel much different from living here in Olympus."

Herbert looked at her with surprise. "Israel is a Jewish country!" he said. "The trees are Jewish, the houses are Jewish, the mountains are Jewish! Christmas isn't even a holiday in Israel!"

Ruthy tried to imagine a place where there was no Christmas. Somehow she couldn't see it at all. She sighed, and poked at a small package in the pile of mail. "What's that?" she asked.

Herbert undid the tissue paper.

"What is it?" Ruthy asked again, for Herbert after unwrapping it, only stood staring at it.

Herbert's cheeks turned pink, and his little-boy chin quivered with excitement. "It's a shaver," he said. His face was filled with awe. "It's an electric shaver!"

A Bar Mitzvah was supposed to celebrate a boy's becoming a man. Ruthy looked at the electric shaver and grinned.

And it was hard to keep from grinning as she sat in the synagogue on Saturday morning and regarded

Herbert standing up there before the Ark. From her seat next to the aisle, Ruthy had a clear view. The Rabbi wore a cap on the back of his head. An embroidered prayer shawl hung over his shoulders.

Herbert, too, wore a small headcovering, and a prayer shawl which had been his grandfather's. It had long fringe. The shawl was so big for Herbert that the fringe on one side almost reached the bottom edge of his new trousers. Ruthy had trouble hiding her smile. Even on his Bar Mitzvah, Herbert was hardly big enough to be much of a man.

Ruthy leaned back and regarded the worshipers around her. They were all dressed up, as she was. All the women wore hats and gloves. Some of the men wore their regular hats instead of the traditional cap. In a synagogue all men kept their heads respectfully covered. She looked around wondering how it would appear to Sandra. Sandra sat primly on an aisle seat just across from Ruthy. She wore her pearls, and she was staring with interest at the round felt derby on the head of the man in the pew in front of her.

Ruthy twitched around in her seat. She guessed Sandra thought it was funny for men to wear hats in the synagogue. In Sandra's church, the men took off their hats.

Ruthy stopped listening to Herbert reciting the prayers in the swaying chant that made her grandmother nod with pride. She put her mind instead on noting the people around her. It was their noses that held her interest. She found one nose even bigger than her father's and viewed it dispassionately, regarding the man in profile. She stared at him intently.

Perhaps the power of her stare was too much for him, for suddenly he turned. And she regarded him in surprise, for the nose was not on the face of a Jew at all. It belonged to Mr. Svenson, the man who ran the fish market. Ruthy had not recognized him all dressed up, without his apron. She smiled broadly.

Then looking the other way she grinned at the thought of her mistake, and stopped when she saw Sandra looking at her. To Sandra going to church was a very serious thing. Sandra was looking at her as if you weren't supposed to smile in church. But then this wasn't a church, Ruthy reflected. Jewish people never called their church a church, they called it a temple or synagogue. This thought, too, made her smile, and this time it was her mother who looked at her with a quick shake of her head. Her mother thought she was not paying attention.

Ruthy looked down at her prayer book, and glanced at the book in her mother's hand. She was several pages behind. She flipped the pages quickly, and they made a rustling sound. Her father, sitting up there on the pulpit holding the Torah Scroll on his lap, looked at her and smiled. Ruthy smiled back. It was perfectly all right to smile in a Jewish synagogue. She guessed Jewish people were very practical that way.

But it would be nice, she thought, to be like Sandra

who didn't seem to think about her religion except on Sunday. When you were Jewish, she reflected, somehow you were Jewish all the time, and not just when you were in a synagogue.

Ruthy began to listen again to the words she had heard Herbert repeat in practice day after day. She said the words inside herself as Herbert said them, and she nodded as he stumbled on one she had remembered perfectly. She knew it better than he did! She looked around. A woman who had come in late sat by herself at the other end of her row. She was still breathless, and on her lap sat a box wrapped in tissue paper and ribbon.

Ruthy blinked as she looked at the package. Her grandmother had said lots of congregations celebrated Bar Mitzvahs for girls. Only they called it a Bas Mitzvah if it was for a girl.

Ruthy twitched at her mother's elbow. "Can I have a Bas Mitzvah?" she whispered.

# 7

"A Bas Mitzvah?" her father said in surprise, when she asked him. "What for?"

"It's just as important for a girl as for a boy!" Ruthy said. Her grandmother nodded.

Her mother said, "Our congregation has never celebrated Bas Mitzvahs for girls."

"But that's no reason why we shouldn't," Ruthy said quickly.

Her mother and father looked at each other doubtfully. Eagerly Ruthy looked from one parent to the other. A whole week had gone by since Herbert's Bar Mitzvah, a week in which the notion had strengthened into a conviction. It seemed to Ruthy that what she wanted most in the whole world was a Bas Mitzvah.

"Forty years ago in England, they were celebrating Bas Mitzvah," her grandmother said, but there was no urgency in her voice. It was as if she were telling them it had rained in the city of Seattle the day before.

Mr. Morgen laid down his newspaper. "Do you know what a Bar Mitzvah means?" he asked Ruthy.

She nodded, uncertainly.

"In the Jewish religion, it isn't necessary to have a temple or synagogue to hold a prayer service. But you have to have ten men. A *minyan,*" he said.

A *minyan,* Ruthy knew, was a Hebrew word.

"When the men gathered to pray, a boy who had become Bar Mitzvah could be counted." He turned to the elder Mrs. Morgen. "Now tell me, in England do they let women count as men?"

Ruthy's grandmother ignored his edge of sarcasm. "So he's old enough for his religious duties," she said casually. "A woman has religious duties too — different ones. A Bar Mitzvah turns a boy into a man, you say. Then a Bas Mitzvah turns a girl into a woman."

Ruthy's mother smiled. "Religiously speaking, that is," she said.

Ruthy didn't see anything to smile about.

Her grandmother shrugged agreeably. "So it's a beginning. For a girl why shouldn't there be a beginning, too?"

"But I'm thinking of our own congregation," Mrs. Morgen said. "Bas Mitzvah for girls is simply not a practice in our own congregation. No one we know of has ever celebrated a Bas Mitzvah. Not to mention the expense," she added.

"But — " Ruthy began, fervently.

"Why don't you go out to play, Ruthy," her father said wearily.

Ruthy opened her mouth, but her mother shook her head, so she went outside and sat on the front steps for a while and then she went back into the house.

"In a way," she said to her father, "it's even more

important for a girl to celebrate a Bas Mitzvah than for a boy to have a Bar Mitzvah. It's the girls who have the babies, isn't it? It's the girls who have to bring their children up Jewish. It's the girls who have the religious responsibility." She nodded, pleased with her arguments.

Her father raised his head from his newspaper. He looked at her foggily. "We'll talk about it later," he mumbled and went back to his reading.

Ruthy went into the kitchen. Her mother was putting away the dishes. "I wouldn't even have to have a new dress," she said eagerly. She had been fitted with a new dress for Herbert's Bar Mitzvah. It was pale blue and had a cording around the waist. "My birthday's not until June and if I grow you can let down the hem," she offered with considered magnanimity.

Her mother looked at her with a perplexed expression. "We'll decide about it later," she said.

Ruthy took heart. She stood there in the middle of the kitchen and pictured herself in her blue dress standing before the congregation, reading faultlessly from the Torah. She wondered, suddenly, whether she should wear gloves while she was reading.

The doorbell rang. Slowly Ruthy moved out of the kitchen through to the front door, and opened it. Mrs. Byrd stood there. Ruthy smiled politely, but for a moment she hadn't known it was Mrs. Byrd. Instead of curlers, she wore a hat, and there was a feather that stuck up out of it. Under her chin was a pinkish silk scarf, and on her hands were gloves.

Mrs. Byrd smiled at her. "Are your parents at home?" she inquired.

Ruthy nodded, aware that behind her in the living room her father was hastily putting on his jacket and looking for his tie.

"Just a minute," she said, and went quickly toward the kitchen. She opened the door a crack. "It's Mrs. Byrd," she whispered loudly. Her mother untied her apron and came hurrying in.

"Come in, come in!" her father was saying heartily to Mrs. Byrd as he held the front door open.

Mrs. Morgen said in her telephone voice, "Well, hello Mrs. Byrd."

Mrs. Byrd apologized. "For dropping in on you like this," she said, as if she usually went only where she was formally invited.

"A neighborly call," she explained as she sat down on the living room sofa and looked brightly around. "Oh my!" she said. "It is nice in here!" As if she hadn't expected to find it nice at all, thought Ruthy.

Mrs. Morgen only smiled.

"Isn't it getting cold!" Mrs. Byrd said, then shivered a little.

Ruthy looked out the window. Most of the trees had dropped their leaves — not the pines and firs and madronas, which were evergreen of course — just the maple trees on this side of the street and the hawthorns around the block on Mrs. Byrd's side. But some of the roses were still blooming. She looked back into the room.

"Well, it's about Christmas I wanted to talk to you," Mrs. Byrd was saying.

"Christmas?" The surprise was there in both the Morgens' voices.

"We haven't even had Thanksgiving yet," Ruthy said.

Mrs. Byrd nodded at her as if she had said a very wise thing. "Exactly!" she said. "And if we expect to accomplish anything at all, we must plan now." She smiled around at all of them.

They waited. Ruthy wondered if perhaps she wanted everyone on the block to celebrate Thanksgiving together. It didn't seem likely. Then she remembered that Mrs. Byrd once had gone around to every house in the neighborhood suggesting they all plant hawthorn trees on the parking strip in front of their houses. Mrs. Byrd already had two hawthorn trees on her parking strip; she thought the whole block should look the same. She finally did get everyone on her street to plant the trees — except Mr. Harvey. He wouldn't even answer his door when she came around.

"Some of us on the block didn't have Christmas lights up last year," Mrs. Byrd confided. "And this

year, if *everyone* cooperates, we might even get the block prize!"

Mr. and Mrs. Morgen looked at each other uneasily.

"Your holly tree will look beautiful with colored lights," Mrs. Byrd exclaimed looking out the window. "That's what everyone has promised to do — put colored lights in at least one tree and an outline on their front door!"

Mr. Morgen cleared his throat.

"We don't celebrate Christmas, you know," Mrs. Morgen explained gently.

"You don't — " Mrs. Byrd laughed as if Mrs. Morgen had just made a joke. "Well, surely you wouldn't mind putting up a few lights?" As she saw Mr. Morgen shaking his head, the incredulity spread to her eyes.

"We are Jews by religion," Mr. Morgen said. "We don't celebrate Christmas."

"No lights?" Mrs. Byrd's eyes opened wider.

"We can put our Hanukah candles in the front window," Mrs. Morgen offered. "It's not exactly the same kind of thing but it's a holiday of ours that comes about the same time as your Christmas and we light candles and exchange gifts to celebrate it."

"Han—" began Mrs. Byrd.

"Hanukah candles," Mrs. Morgen said easily.

Mrs. Byrd seemed nonplussed. Mrs. Morgen chattered gaily as she ushered her to the front door, although Mrs. Byrd didn't seem to have much to say. "But it's a community project," she put in a little weakly.

Mrs. Byrd was supposed to be very civic-minded, Ruthy recalled.

Mrs. Morgen smiled. "I'll put lots of Hanukah candles in the window," she said. "Eight of them."

Ruthy stood by the window and watched Mrs. Byrd go down the walk and cross the street. She watched her ring the doorbell of Mrs. Hudson's house, and watched too as the two women stood and talked. Their mouths went up and down, and so did Mrs. Byrd's hands.

Ruthy was still there looking out the window when both Mrs. Byrd and Mrs. Hudson stared across the street at her house. Then Ruthy turned away, walked through the house, and out the back door.

# 8

MR. HARVEY was burning up some old cartons in the alley. Ruthy contemplated him from her back porch, wondering whether he was going to string up colored lights for Mrs. Byrd. She walked through the yard, opened the back gate and closed it behind her.

"Mrs. Byrd is out getting everybody to put up Christmas lights," she told him.

Mr. Harvey glanced at Ruthy. "Hummph," he said. He poked another piece of carton into the old garbage can which held his fire.

"Are you going to decorate the way she wants you to?" Ruthy looked at him with interest.

Mr. Harvey stopped. "I don't celebrate Christmas," he said.

Ruthy looked at him closely. "You mean you don't believe in Christmas either?" she asked.

"That's what I told her." Mr. Harvey went on throwing trash into the smoking can. "I told her as far as she was concerned I don't believe in anything. Not anything at all. I'm a non-believer, that's what I told her."

Ruthy went on down the alley toward Sandra's house. Marguerite's house was separated from San-

dra's by a white picket fence. Every Christmas, Marguerite's father outlined the whole roof edge with strings of colored lights. Once he had even put a big cardboard Santa up there, sticking out of the chimney. Marguerite's high voice came from Sandra's backyard. Ruthy paused at the back gate there.

"Hi!" she called.

The two girls sat together on Sandra's back porch.

"Hi," said Sandra crisply. Marguerite nodded, exchanged glances with Sandra and smiled secretly.

Ruthy came slowly toward them. It seemed to her that already she could smell Christmas in the air. Every year Sandra and Marguerite always made a great fuss about exchanging Christmas presents, and Ruthy always pretended it had nothing to do with her and that it didn't matter much anyway. Ruthy sat down with them, but it was not three together. It was more like two and one. Ruthy felt it even though she didn't know whether or not the others did. Feeling their eyes upon her she looked off down the alley toward Mr. Harvey's house.

"Mr. Harvey doesn't believe in anything," she said, idly.

Her statement seemed to electrify them.

"You mean he's an atheist!" The horror was in Sandra's face.

Rather pleased with the unexpected stir she had made, Ruthy shrugged. "Something like that," she said. "He's burning leaves and stuff in his alley now."

Marguerite, a peculiar excitement in her voice, said, "Maybe it's not leaves at all! Maybe it's a sacrifice or something!"

Sandra jumped up. "Let's go see!"

Uneasily Ruthy stood up with them. "I'm sure it's nothing like that," she mumbled. She began to realize she didn't exactly know what a non-believer was.

Sandra moved quickly to her side and thrust her arm into Ruthy's. "Did you notice anything especially peculiar?" she said.

Ruthy shook her head firmly. "Not especially," she said.

Marguerite took her other arm. "I wouldn't be surprised if there was something *very* peculiar," she said positively.

They walked like that, one on each side of her down the alley, each clinging to Ruthy, as if each liked her best.

Then they decided not to march straight down the alley but to cut through one of the yards and sneak into Ruthy's backyard and view the situation from behind the Morgens' fence.

But after all the maneuvering, it turned out to be a little disappointing. Mr. Harvey had already gone back into his house. The fire in the trash can had gone out. The only evidence of the burning was a bad smell.

Ruthy stood up. Mr. Harvey lifted his window shade to see whether the can's contents were still burning, and saw her. He smiled at Ruthy and lowered the shade again.

"Let's run out, and kick over the can, and run back again," Sandra proposed.

Marguerite jumped up, ready.

"No!" said Ruthy.

They looked at her in surprise.

"I mean," she said, "that's sort of kid stuff. To my way of thinking, that is."

Standing together, they looked at her warily.

"Besides — " Ruthy said, talking fast, improvising, "I came over to tell you something."

"What?" said Sandra, her face turned unfriendly.

Ruthy ignored it. "It's about a party," she said. She flopped down on the grass and leaned back against the trunk of the cherry tree.

Somewhat reluctantly Sandra sat down, and Marguerite too.

"You're going to give a party?"

Ruthy looked toward her house. Her grandmother, moving hurriedly, as she always did, with short quick steps, could be seen passing the window.

"It's my Bas Mitzvah," said Ruthy. "I'm going to have a Bas Mitzvah."

Carefully Ruthy closed the kitchen door behind her. She stood there a moment thinking of how she had just told Sandra and Marguerite that she was going to have a Bas Mitzvah. She grimaced as she thought of how she had made it sound as if a Bas Mitzvah was better than three Christmases all rolled together. It was funny, but they had believed her.

Her grandmother smiled at her. Ruthy's mouth twisted in answer. Her mother looked up from the kitchen table where she was sitting making out a grocery list. Mr. Morgen came in at that moment from the other room and went directly to the refrigerator.

"I told them!" Ruthy said. Her voice sounded hollow.

Her father snagged a green onion from the vegetable drawer and turned about. "You told who what?" he asked twinkling at her. He held the onion between his teeth and closed the refrigerator door.

Ruthy unbuttoned her coat and pulled her scarf back off her head. She faced them all feeling a flutter in her throat.

"I told Marguerite and Sandra I was going to have a Bas Mitzvah."

The green onion tail hung from her father's mouth as he stared at her. Her mother put her pencil down, and her grandmother began to look worried.

"Did I say you could?" her father asked.

"You didn't say I couldn't!" Ruthy said quickly. And then pressed her upper teeth over her under lip.

Her father regarded her with asperity. "If a person doesn't say no it means yes?" he said.

Ruthy shook her head. Once when she was very small her father had taken the belt off his trousers and given her three whacks on her bottom for doing something she no longer even remembered. All she remembered was the sound of that strap. She took a step backward.

But her father only looked at her, and in the looking his expression changed. "Ruthy," he said softly, "does it really mean so much to you?"

Ruthy raised her head, and nodded quickly, but if he had asked her the reason why, she couldn't have answered.

Her father looked at her mother. "We were waiting to talk to the Rabbi, Ruthy," her mother said. "We had decided that if the Rabbi is willing to spend the time to teach you, there is no reason why you shouldn't have a Bas Mitzvah — if you really want it."

Ruthy felt the tears spurt from her eyes. "I'm sorry," she cried. Hiding her tear-blobbed face with her arm she ran out of the kitchen and upstairs to her room. She threw herself down on her bed and sobbed loudly. But exactly what it was she was sorry for, she did not know.

# 9

THEY walked with their arms around each other, down the street, all the way to Ruthy's house. Sandra had walked home with Ruthy every day the last two weeks, walking all the way down the block with her, not turning off at the corner which was the shortest way to Sandra's house.

"I guess we won't have as much time as this after the first of the year, when I have to study for my Bas Mitzvah." Ruthy sighed elaborately. The Rabbi had agreed to begin lessons for Ruthy in January. Her Bas Mitzvah ceremony had been set for March, a little early considering that her birthday was not until June. Hers would be early; but then Herbert's had been held late.

It had been decided that Ruthy's Bas Mitzvah would take place at the Friday evening service rather than Saturday morning which was traditional for the Bar Mitzvah service. After the service there would be a reception and cookies and punch. Ruthy's grandmother was already beginning to bake for that!

"Do you think you'll get as many things as Herbert did?" Sandra asked eagerly. She had never seen as many gifts as Herbert had received, she had confided to Ruthy after the Bar Mitzvah.

"I'm not supposed to think about the gifts," Ruthy said, suddenly feeling righteous.

"Why not?"

"It isn't like a regular birthday," Ruthy tried to explain. "It's more significant. You're not supposed to care about things like that at a Bas Mitzvah. I mean, that's not what really counts."

"What counts?" Sandra asked.

"Well, being old enough to be considered grown up. And all that."

"You mean your mother and father will treat you like a grownup as soon as you've had your Bas Mitzvah?" Sandra sounded impressed.

"I guess they're supposed to," Ruthy said, although privately she was a little doubtful. So far as she could see they didn't treat Herbert any differently. No so you could notice it, that is.

"I don't think my mother will ever treat me like a grownup," Sandra said. "She thinks I don't even think about boys."

Ruthy looked at her with interest. "Do you?"

"Do I what?"

"Think about boys?"

Sandra giggled. "Do you?"

"There's no law against thinking," Ruthy said smiling broadly.

They glanced at each other from between their eyelashes and giggled some more.

Suddenly Sandra grew serious. "That's the trouble with Marguerite," she said.

Breathlessly Ruthy drew a little closer.

"Boys," said Sandra. "Boys like her."

"You call that trouble?" said Ruthy.

Sandra giggled again. "No, what I mean is, she knows it. She's always talking about boys. Honestly, it makes me sick sometimes. She never even thinks of anything else."

Ruthy grinned at Sandra. "You mean there *is* something else?" she inquired.

And then Herbert came walking down the street in that stiff-legged stride he had used since his Bar Mitzvah, and stopped to stare at them.

"What's so funny?" he asked.

Ruthy looked at Sandra and Sandra looked at Herbert and suddenly Sandra stuffed the edge of her scarf into her mouth. She made a big thing about holding back her laughter.

"Nothing," said Ruthy quickly, frowning at him. But Sandra wasn't frowning at all. She took the scarf away from her face and looked at Herbert through her eyelashes. Herbert looked straight back at her.

"Be seeing you," he said jauntily and strode up the walk to the house.

Sandra turned to look after him.

Ruthy picked up her books from where she had laid them on the step. "Well, goodbye," she said.

Sandra smiled at her, brilliantly . . . But it wasn't

for her, Ruthy could see. It was for Herbert, who was standing at the living room window pretending to look out but really looking at Sandra.

"I'll come over a little later," Ruthy said.

Sandra, with studied effect, picked up her books. "If you feel like it, you can bring Herbert," she said casually.

Ruthy stood and watched her move down the street, taking unnecessarily short steps. Her bottom wiggled as she walked, and standing in the window, Herbert grinned.

Ruthy rushed up the steps to the door and slammed it behind her.

# 10

Ruthy slid off the counter stool in the drugstore and waited, looking at the Christmas tree ornaments, while Sandra went up to the cash register to pay for their sundaes. Both girls loved sundaes, and they had eaten them with ritualistic deliberation, making the hot chocolate sauce last down to the final spoonful of ice cream.

"Remember, mum's the word," Sandra said as they let the glass door swing behind them.

Ruthy glanced at Sandra. Every day for a week now Sandra had stood treats for sundaes. Every day she had left Ruth with the same caution. *Mum's the word.* The phrase had unpleasant memories. Ruthy made a face. "What's so mum about it?" she asked.

Sandra looked at her quickly and then away. "Well, frankly, it's my mother."

"Doesn't she want you to eat sundaes?"

"Oh, she doesn't care how many sundaes I eat. It's the money. She'd be mad if she knew I was spending this money on sundaes."

Ruthy shrugged. "Well, it's your money, isn't it?"

Sandra didn't answer.

They walked down the dark street toward their block. It was a blue black evening when the cold air seemed to make the lights even shinier. Their street looked lovely, thought Ruthy. Almost every doorway was outlined with Christmas lights, and the trees in front of the houses glimmered blue, green and red. Only her own house at the end of the block stood dark and silent. Even the Hanukah candles in the window didn't make much of a show.

"It's almost Christmas," said Sandra.

"I know." Ruthy wished her house didn't look so glum standing there, as if it didn't belong.

"I just love Christmas!" Sandra said.

Ruthy didn't say anything.

"Don't you?" Sandra gave a little skip. "Don't you just love Christmas?"

"It's a very pretty time of the year," Ruthy said primly. "The lights and all, I mean."

Sandra looked at her quizzically.

"It's not exactly part of our religion," Ruthy said.

Sandra stopped. "You mean you don't really believe in Christmas? I mean, really?"

"Not if you're Jewish," Ruthy said.

Sandra said, "When I was little, I thought the whole world was Christian. I mean, I couldn't imagine anyone not being Christian, if you know what I mean."

Ruthy made a face. "Yeah, I know what you mean." She reflected that it had seemed that way to her too.

"What does Herbert think?" Sandra asked suddenly as they neared the house.

Ruthy looked at her in surprise. "About what?"

"About Christmas, and all that," Sandra said lightly.

Ruthy gave her friend a quick look. "Well, you know, he's Jewish too," she said.

"Oh," said Sandra. And she laughed, an odd laugh. As if she had never thought about Herbert being Jewish. Ruthy looked at her curiously.

Closing the front door behind her, Ruthy stood still a moment in the dimly lit hallway. Every house on the block but hers had a Christmas tree, she thought, and glanced into the orderly living room. Her mother had placed a holly branch in a vase on the fireplace mantel. Ruthy made a face. She tried to imagine what it would be like to come in and see a lighted Christmas tree in the corner by the fireplace. She half-closed her eyes, squinting into the gloom of the living room. But it was no good. She sighed. The one thing she just couldn't imagine was a Christmas tree in the Morgens' living room.

"Anybody home?" she called as she went on through the hallway. There was no one in the kitchen either. Prince, hearing her voice, thumped his tail on the porch outside. Ruthy opened the door and let him in. She looked at him feeling the usual impatience.

"You're not much of a prince," she said. She regarded him critically. "On the other hand, you're not even a respectable pauper," she pointed out. "You're too fat."

Prince blinked, and then he yawned.

Ruthy laughed. "I guess you're just a *hoont,*" she said. She allowed him to follow her upstairs to her room.

Sitting on her bed, she stared out the window. The holly tree loomed outside there. She tried to imagine it decked with colored lights. "I guess you'd like to see it with colored lights too, wouldn't you?" she asked him. Prince yawned. Ruthy sat there watching him yawn.

"You don't know how lucky you are," she said. "You're not Jewish or Christian or anything. If you were Mrs. Byrd's dog, you'd be wearing silver bells on your collar and have lights around your doghouse roof."

Prince sat up, his eyes gleaming. Ruthy sat up too. Slowly she moved off the bed. She went to her jewel box which was on top of her chest of drawers and removed her coin purse. She counted the quarters and dimes in it. There was slightly over $1.50. Thoughtfully, she looked out the window. It would be easy to cut a branch of holly, she decided, and she could walk down to the variety store and buy a little string of colored lights and a box of tinsel.

Putting the money inside her mitten, she went downstairs. She heard her grandmother moving

around in the kitchen. Quickly Ruthy opened the front door and ran up the street.

Ruthy hid the package of decorations in the garage before she came into the house. She had decided that she would cut a little pine branch, instead of the holly, and she wouldn't bring the tree into the house at all. She would decorate it in the garage. That way it would be more the dog's tree.

Her hands and feet were cold when she finished decorating the tree the next day. It stood up sturdily, planted in an empty pickle jar which she had camouflaged in silver foil. Inside the jar was a good practical base of rocks and sand, dug from the edge of the alley.

The tree made quite a respectable showing, she thought proudly. She had hung tinsel on it with care, and tied to its branches little silver balls. She stared at it, frowning a little. Most trees, she remembered, had a star of Bethlehem on the top. Thoughtfully she looked at her tree. The star of Bethlehem was Jesus' star. On an impulse she took the roll of foil and tore off a sheet. She turned it this way and that, making it several thicknesses through, and then folded it carefully into a six-pointed star.

"There!" she said, and placed it on the tip of the tree. She grinned. A six-pointed star was a Jewish star, a star of David. She guessed it wouldn't make any difference to a dog, anyway. She stood back and looked at it proudly.

"Here Prince!" Ruthy shouted, sticking her head out of the garage door. Prince sat on the back porch, happily playing with the soupbone Ruthy's grandmother had just set out for him. He didn't pay any attention to her summons.

"Come here! Prince!" Ruthy called loudly. She tried whistling at him, then looked back to view her handiwork. The star of David was quite pretty, she had at first thought. Now, suddenly, she frowned at it.

Her feet were cold when she stamped up the back

steps. Waiting a moment just outside the kitchen door, she listened to the voices inside.

"It was Sandra," Herbert was saying. He must have been talking with her over the telephone. "They're decorating their Christmas tree and she's making popcorn and wants me to come over and help her eat it."

Ruthy entered the kitchen hastily. "You mean you're going over to Sandra's?"

"Sure!" he said. "Why not? She invited me."

"To help decorate her Christmas tree?" Ruthy's voice rang out accusingly.

Herbert looked at her pityingly. "Look, I'm just going over to eat her popcorn, not to marry her."

Mrs. Morgen looked shocked. Mr. Morgen only grinned. Her grandmother looked loudly disapproving. Her grandmother never *said* anything when she didn't like what was going on. But she might just as well have, Ruthy thought.

"I don't see why you bother," Ruthy said, as if it didn't make any difference to her.

"But I like popcorn," Herbert said innocently.

Herbert opened the door. He paused. "Oh, by the way, she said I could bring you if I wanted to."

Ruthy hesitated. But only for a moment. "Why not?" she said, and buttoned up her coat again.

She walked with him through the backyard, past Mr. Harvey's house, and down the alley. Herbert whistled. He walked with his hands in his pockets and whistled. Her own fingers were cold even with her mittens on.

"Shut up," she said.

He stopped. "Look," he began, talking quickly. "Sandra asked me to go to the show with her tomorrow afternoon."

She shrugged. "So go."

"She's got this sort of cousin staying with her." Herbert grimaced. "He's a *goy*, if you know what I mean."

Ruthy looked at him quickly. She knew exactly what he meant.

Suddenly he seemed a little embarrassed. "But if he asks you to go and you want to — well, I'll be there."

A pleasant little warmth trickled down to Ruthy's fingertips. "Maybe I won't want to go," she said, offhandedly.

Herbert eyed her with what seemed like uncertainty. "Her mother won't let her go unless he goes too."

"Oh," said Ruthy. She didn't look at Herbert. He wanted her to be the decoy. That's all he was thinking about. He wanted her to go along with this other boy so that Sandra's mother wouldn't know that Sandra was really going with Herbert and not with her cousin. It was hardly what you'd call a tempting invitation, she thought. "I'll let you know," she said. They turned into Sandra's yard.

Sandra squeezed her hand as she greeted Ruthy and Herbert at the door. It was supposed to be significant, Ruthy thought. Everything Sandra did lately had taken on an aura of significance. Like Sandra treating her to sundaes every day after school and being so secretive about it. And talking about boys in general, but really meaning Herbert. And preferring Ruthy's company all of a sudden instead of Marguerite's. Marguerite didn't have a brother.

Ruthy laid her hat and coat on Sandra's bed and came out of the bedroom with a smile pasted on her face.

"Oh, Ruthy," said Mrs. Wright, and looked surprised.

She's wondering why Sandra asked us, thought Ruthy. "Your tree is beautiful," Ruthy said politely.

Mrs. Wright smiled. "How nice of you to come over and enjoy it with us," she said.

Ruthy grimaced inside. Mrs. Wright always talked to her as if she were an orphan, she thought suddenly. She wondered suddenly how an orphan was supposed to act. She opened her eyes wide and stared at Mrs. Wright. "We've never had a Christmas tree," she said.

Mrs. Wright patted her shoulder comfortingly. "I know, dear," she said. "How would you like to hang some more of this tinsel on ours?" she suggested generously.

Ruthy took the tinsel dutifully and carried it over

to the tree. It had too much tinsel on it already, she thought. She laid the whole blob of it on a low branch where it wouldn't be seen.

"Hey," said a boy popping up from the other side of the tree. He looked as if his shirt were buttoned too tightly under his neck. "Don't you even know how to trim a Christmas tree!" He removed the blob and began to separate the strands.

Ruthy stared at him. This must be the cousin.

"Can't say that I do," she said.

"You mean you've never trimmed a Christmas tree?" He was so surprised he stopped plucking at the strands.

"I'm Jewish," Ruthy said, folding her arms across her chest.

Sandra came up in a little rush. "Oh, Clyde," she panted, "this is Ruthy, Herbert's sister. Ruthy, this is my cousin, Clyde."

"Oh," said Clyde. He stared at Ruthy frankly. She stared back.

"You don't look Jewish," he said finally. And smiled.

Ruthy said, "You don't look Christian," and didn't smile at all.

His face grew red. Ruthy watched it get that way. It started where his shirt collar creased into his neck and moved slowly up his cheeks. A shade being pulled up from the bottom, instead of down from the top, she thought, and smiled.

"Whew!" he said, grinning now all over his red face. "For a minute, I thought you were going to hit me."

Ruthy laughed. "For a minute," she admitted, "I almost did."

Herbert's worried face floated at her from the other side of the room. He saw her smile, and he smiled too.

She guessed she would go to the show, she decided. But she pretended she couldn't make up her mind when Clyde asked her, and she walked home with Herbert, humming, her head up, her fingers warm and tingly, because after all, say what you will about the circumstances, it was really her first date.

# II

THE telephone rang almost as soon as Ruthy and Herbert reached home. It was Sandra.

"Just a minute," Ruthy said. She waited until Herbert left the kitchen and tramped upstairs.

"What do you think of him?" Sandra asked cozily.

"You mean Clyde?" Ruthy said. She hadn't thought of him much at all.

Sandra laughed, a tinkly little laugh.

"Of course I mean Clyde. He thinks you're all right."

Ruthy said wryly, "Well, I guess he's all right too."

"Yes, I know. But what do you think of him? Really I mean."

Ruthy hesitated. She said instead, "Herbert's talked of nothing else but taking you to the show tomorrow." It was perfectly true, Ruthy decided. He hadn't really talked of anything else. There hadn't been time.

"Really?" Sandra said, sighing.

"Really," Ruthy said.

"Isn't it funny how he's been around all my life practically, and I never even noticed him before?"

Ruthy tried to see something unusual about that

but couldn't quite find it. "After all, he's only thirteen," she pointed out.

"Well, I think he's very mature for his age. Don't you think so?"

"I don't know," Ruthy said. She made a face. "He's always seemed pretty young to me — even though he is older — older than me, I mean."

"It must be nice having an older brother — like Herbert, I mean." Sandra sighed again.

"Yeah," said Ruthy. Her arm was beginning to twitch. "I guess so."

Sandra laughed. "Y'know, it was only a year ago that I thought he was just a child. Isn't that funny? I never dreamed he would turn out like this."

"Like what?" Ruthy asked, really curious.

"So *serious,*" Sandra said. "As if he's thinking about things all the time. And the way he suddenly looks off into the distance, and gets completely lost in his thoughts."

Ruthy sighed. Not the same kind of sigh as Sandra's. "Could be he's just inventorying his Bar Mitzvah gifts," she suggested. "You know, he remembers every one he got and who gave it to him."

"Isn't that wonderful!" Sandra said.

Ruthy looked at the telephone. She hadn't meant it that way. She tried to change the subject. "What are you going to wear tomorrow?"

"Tomorrow? I haven't decided. What's Herbert's favorite color?"

Ruthy grinned. "Puce," she said.

"What!" It was a shriek.

"It's just something Herbert says he likes. It's the color of the exhaust or whatever you call it that comes from a rocket."

There was a moment of silence on the other end of the line. Then Sandra laughed.

"Oh, I see," she said. "That's supposed to be funny. Seriously, does he have any feeling about blue?"

Ruthy scratched her nose. "Well, I can ask him, if you want me to."

"Oh no!" Sandra said. "Don't ask him. But find out for me, will you?"

Doubtfully, Ruthy suggested, "He's never said anything about not liking my blue sweater dress, if that's what you mean. To tell you the truth," she added, "he never tells me what he likes, just what he doesn't like."

Sandra's laugh tinkled out again. "That's because you're his sister," she said. "Now Clyde loves pink."

"I don't look good in pink," Ruthy said quickly.

"Well, why don't you wear the blue then."

"Okay," Ruthy said. She didn't see how it would make much difference one way or another. They were only going to a show, and when she took off her coat in the theater, it would be too dark to see what color she wore.

"I'll wear blue, too," Sandra said. "And my Christmas pearls. I'm going to wash my hair tonight, and put polish on my fingernails. My mother has the prettiest silvery polish. It's pink, but it's silver too. And I'm getting perfume for Christmas." She asked, suddenly anxious, "Does Herbert like perfume?"

Ruthy grinned. "He's never worn any," she said, and said goodbye quickly before Sandra would get mad.

"The movie is all about rockets," Ruthy heard Herbert explaining to Sandra as they walked ahead on the way to the theater. They stopped outside the movie house and examined the marquee.

Herbert stood, his hands in his pockets, gazing at the poster beside the box office. Ruthy waited at Clyde's side as he bought two tickets, and Sandra nudged Herbert's arm a little impatiently.

"Come on!" she said. "Everybody is waiting for you."

Herbert counted out his change, his eyes wandering back to the poster.

"It really could land on the moon," he said to Clyde. "I read in the papers that it wasn't a fake at all. That it's an exact model being tested."

"Wow!" said Clyde.

"I hope we can get good seats," said Herbert as they entered the lobby.

The usher smiled at him. "How many?"

"Four!" said Clyde importantly. It was dark in the lobby, and he took Ruthy's hand. His hand was sticky, thought Ruthy, but she didn't pull hers away. She thought it wouldn't be polite.

"All I can give you is three together and one single," the girl said.

Sandra and Ruthy looked at each other. Herbert who had been standing there peering at the screen through the curtains wasn't paying any attention. Ruthy poked at him with her elbow.

"She can only give us three together and one single," she said in a loud whisper.

Herbert looked around. "Okay," he said. "I'll take the single." He moved after the usher as she guided him down the aisle with her small flashlight beam.

Sandra looked mad. She followed Ruthy and Clyde down the aisle and plopped into her seat. Then she sat up on its edge and looked around the movie house to see where Herbert was sitting.

"Do you see him?" Ruthy whispered, looking too.

"Who?" asked Sandra.

"Herbert."

Sandra sat back. "I wasn't even looking for him," she said. But Ruthy knew she had been, for she suddenly spied him herself. He was sitting on an aisle seat, his eyes glued to the screen.

"He's crazy about rockets," Ruthy whispered to Sandra.

Sandra endowed her with a bitter look. "You said it, he's crazy all right."

The show was all right, thought Ruthy. Anyway,

Clyde became so interested he kept his sticky hands clasped in his lap, and Sandra's fidgeting soon lapsed into a normal amount of wiggling.

"We mustn't forget Herbert," Sandra said as they moved up the aisle at the show's end.

She's decided to be sweet about it, Ruthy thought, and took her friend's arm.

"We'll wait for him out front," Ruthy said.

They stood there, close to the box office, talking about the picture, jostled by the people coming out and standing and blinking. They talked and they laughed. Sandra giggled a lot, keeping her eye on the people coming out.

And suddenly the lobby inside was empty. They stood there, uncertainly, watching the doorman unhook the double doors and let them close.

"Maybe he's in the — " Clyde began. He went quickly back into the lobby.

Ruthy and Sandra waited outside, buttoning their coats up tight to their necks and pretending nothing was unusual. When Clyde came out, alone, they started to walk home.

"Sure funny," Clyde said.

"Do you think something could have happened to him?" Sandra said. "Maybe he got sick or something."

Ruthy said, more to comfort Sandra than because it was really so, "He gets sick awfully quickly sometimes." She snapped her fingers. "Just like that, sometimes."

They walked on slowly, crossed the street, and turned the corner.

"Hey!" said Clyde, pointing. "Who's that?"

Ahead of them, halfway down the block, strolling along, was Herbert.

Sandra gasped, and Ruthy shouted, "Herbert!"

He turned. They saw his mouth open as he gazed upon the three of them. They hurried toward him.

He struck his forehead with the palm of his hand. "Oh my gosh!" he said. "I forgot!"

"You forgot!" Sandra's voice rose to a shriek.

"Y'see, I always go to the matinee by myself," he tried to explain. "And when the lights went on, I just got up and walked out, as usual." He turned to Clyde. "Boy!" he said. "Wasn't that some rocket, though. Did you notice the take-off! Phewwwwwww!" he whistled through his teeth, sweeping the air with his hand.

"Do you think they really could land on the moon with a rig like that?" Clyde asked him.

"Sure!" said Herbert. "Why not?"

The two boys walked together, talking excitedly, making motions with their hands and odd sounds through their teeth. Sandra and Ruthy followed along behind, together.

When they reached Sandra's house, Sandra ran up the steps and slammed the door. But neither Clyde nor Herbert noticed. They were still talking about retro rockets, orbiting stations, and gravitational fields.

Ruthy walked on by herself, through Sandra's backyard, down the alley, past Mr. Harvey's house. There was a new sign tacked on Mrs. Byrd's fence. Curiously she stopped to look at it. NO TRESPASSING, it said. It was a funny place for a sign, thought Ruthy as she went through her own backyard and into her house.

# 12

Ruthy ran into the alley. Mr. Harvey smiled at her. Even the cats stared at her with friendly interest.

"Hi, Mr. Harvey!" she called.

He waved, standing in his doorway with a sweater buttoned up under his chin. There was an old scarf tied around his neck, too.

Mrs. Byrd's back door opened. She stuck her head out. "I warn you!" she shouted at Mr. Harvey. "If I catch your cats trespassing on my property, I'll call the Humane Society to pick them up!"

Mr. Harvey only picked up his broom, swept the stoop and went back into the house again.

It was New Year's Day. Mrs. Byrd's discarded Christmas tree, stripped of its decorations but still stiffly green, lay next to her garbage can. Ruthy waved at Mrs. Byrd, too, although her gesture was as much to stretch her arms as anything else. For she had been sitting all morning munching cookies and reviewing her Hebrew textbook. She could read very well in Hebrew, Ruthy thought proudly. Of course, she didn't understand much of what she was reading, but she liked the strange sound of the words and she read aloud with expression as if she really did know the meaning.

In her Sunday school, they taught you first to read the Hebrew letters and then to say the sounds properly before they taught you the meanings of the words. It wasn't the way they taught French or Spanish in regular school, Ruthy reflected, but perhaps that was because the Hebrew language had an alphabet of its own. *Aleph, bet, gimel, dalet* — she recited the first letters of the Hebrew alphabet as she hurried along.

For her Bas Mitzvah, the Rabbi had told her, she would learn some special Hebrew prayers, both in Hebrew and in English. Someday, she decided, perhaps she would learn how to speak Hebrew the way they spoke it in Israel. Someday she would like to go to Israel . . . and to China, and Italy and France — she interrupted herself with a laugh. The truth was she wanted to go everywhere, and see everything. She turned into Sandra's backyard.

"Happy New Year!" she called out loudly. That was one of the holidays that had nothing to do with religion, she thought happily. Everyone celebrated New Year's. And if you were Jewish you celebrated it twice. Once on December 31, and once in September which was the Jewish New Year, calculated by the moon instead of the sun.

"Hi!" she said then to Sandra who had just come out her back door, and she smiled. She had not seen Sandra since Herbert had forgotten her at the show. She giggled, thinking of it. Sandra would think it was funny by now, too. "What's new?" Ruthy called out.

But Sandra only looked at her coldly. "I can't play with you anymore," Sandra said, looking over the top of Ruthy's head.

Ruthy stopped.

"My mother says I'd better not see you anymore at all." And she looked back at her door as if her mother might be standing there now.

Ruthy looked at her uncertainly. She said — "Herbert didn't mean . . ."

Sandra jerked her head around. "Oh, it has nothing to do with Herbert!" she said. She gave a light little laugh. "Who cares about Herbert?" She sniffed. "He's only a child."

"Oh," said Ruthy, and waited.

"It's you I'm not supposed to play with. To tell you the truth — " she looked over her shoulder again as if she wanted to make sure she wasn't overheard — "I shouldn't even be talking to you now. My mother said the only one in this neighborhood I can play with is Marguerite. She said from now on I'd better stick to my own kind." And Sandra turned about, flipping her skirt a little, went into her house and closed the door firmly behind her.

Ruthy walked back down the alley. She felt a tightness inside her somewhat the way she felt after a cold when her chest hurt and every breath hurt a little. She didn't turn into her own backyard but kept right on walking, across the street, through the next alley, and across the street through another one. Little children playing in their backyards looked at her curiously. One woman, hanging out her clothes, nodded at her. Ruthy wondered if she knew she was Jewish. Then she turned around and walked back home.

"Hi pickleface!" Herbert said gaily as she entered the warm kitchen, and his face turned surprised when she strode straight toward him.

"Get out of my way!" she said in a low voice. The words seemed thick in her throat.

He stood there, in the middle of the kitchen, his hands in his pockets and his elbows sticking out. He stood there daring her.

She pushed him, and he pushed back. She bent her head and rammed into him.

"Hey!" he shouted, sitting on the floor. "You cut that out!" and added, "Pickleface!"

Ruthy jumped on him then, sitting on his stomach, holding him down.

"Help!" Herbert shouted. "Help!" but he wasn't fighting very hard, she saw, and he was only pretending he couldn't get up.

She stood up, and looked down at him pretending to be writhing in pain down on the floor. Her grandmother came hurrying in. Herbert got up. He smiled.

"Hi Grandma," he said, as if nothing had been going on at all, and he ambled out of the kitchen.

"Shame!" the grandmother called after him.

"Shame! A boy who has had his Bar Mitzvah already." But she looked most severely at Ruthy. "It's not nice for a Jewish girl to fight like a boy," she said.

Ruthy straightened her skirt. She sniffed. "Whoever asked me if I wanted to be Jewish?" she said.

Her grandmother shrugged. "Who's to ask?"

Ruthy stood there watching her as she took the two brass candlesticks from the cupboard and placed them on the kitchen table. On Friday evening at sundown, her grandmother lit the Sabbath candles. Silently Ruthy watched.

She knew the words by heart herself although she had never consciously learned them: *Boruch atah adonay* . . . Blessed art thou O Lord our God . . . Her grandmother recited the prayer with her hands over her eyes. When she was finished she withdrew

her hands and smiled at Ruthy. "Good Sabbath," she said.

Ruthy gazed at the candle flame. She had never known her grandmother to miss lighting the candles on a Friday night. It was as much a part of her Friday evening as chicken soup.

"So what if you don't light the candles one Friday night?" Ruthy said.

Her grandmother looked at her severely. "A promise is a promise," she said.

She meant keeping the Sabbath was the promise the Jewish people had made to God. Ruthy guessed she had known that. But she had never thought about it much.

Ruthy sighed. She guessed she could get along without Sandra just as well as Sandra could get along without her. Thinking of Sandra, she winced involuntarily.

"When I'm old enough to go out, I'm going out with only Jewish boys," Ruthy announced halfway through dinner.

"Pass the potato latkes," her father said, as if she hadn't said anything very important. But her grandmother halted the platter to put an extra pancake on Ruthy's plate before passing it on.

Her mother looked at her closely before saying, "We have a little time yet before we have to worry about that."

Herbert, his mouth full, chewed thoughtfully, gazing at her. She pretended her decision had nothing to do with Sandra, but she knew she wasn't fooling Herbert. She wasn't fooling him one bit.

He cornered her, after dinner, and barred her way up the stairs. "What happened?"

"Nothing happened." She fixed him with a sure look.

"Okay, then, what did Clyde say?"

She said, "Clyde? I wasn't even thinking of Clyde."

"Sandra then," Herbert said. "Did you and Sandra have a fight?"

"I didn't have any fight with Sandra," she said offhandedly, stressing the "I" very slightly.

He looked at her a moment, but he didn't let her by.

"She said something about me, didn't she?"

Ruthy grinned. "She said you were a *child.*" She pronounced the words with relish.

He stepped aside then, and let her go on up. But he stood there watching her mount the stairs, and he didn't move until she had reached the landing above and opened the door into her room.

# 13

THE Rabbi was sitting at his desk when Ruthy knocked at the door of his study. He was writing and didn't look up when she came in.

"Sit down, a minute, Ruthy," he said, not even glancing at her.

Ruthy sat down. The Rabbi wore his little black skullcap on the back of his head. She had hardly noticed it at first. It was only when he turned that she saw it there. He didn't look like a Rabbi, she thought, or at least not the way you'd think a Rabbi would look. He wasn't thin and round shouldered, and highbrowed and intense, and he didn't walk with his hands tucked behind him, or wear a beard like the Jews in the paintings on the wall in the vestibule of the synagogue. He looked like anybody else.

Her glance strayed to the wall where several black and gold framed diplomas hung. He was a Doctor of Philosophy, one certified. Another said Doctor of Law. Ruthy felt surprised. He didn't look that smart. Somehow she had always expected all doctors and professors to talk like her language arts teacher. But the Rabbi talked like her Aunt Ada who came from New York.

The Rabbi put down his pen. "Now," he said.

"Tell me, why do you want to become Bas Mitzvah?"

Ruthy asked in a hurry because she really wanted to know, "Why did you become a Rabbi?"

Startled at first by the abruptness of her question, Rabbi Hazman sat back and laughed. "That puts me in mind of a story," he said. He stared at the ceiling a moment and smiled. "Once there was a Jew who was asked by an irate judge, 'Why do you always answer a question with a question?' And the Jew shrugged and answered, 'Why not?' "

Ruthy laughed. "I wasn't trying to answer your question," she said. "I was just thinking about something else."

"Well, maybe you think about this a little, hmmm?" the Rabbi suggested. "And then later you tell me."

Ruthy nodded.

"It is good to question," he said. "That's what Judaism believes. First to question, then to study, then to learn." He sat there a moment staring again at the ceiling. "It is not too much to learn," he said, almost as if he were talking to himself. He looked at Ruthy. "You like stories?"

"Who doesn't like stories?" Ruthy answered and they laughed together.

"Once there was a great Rabbi named Hillel." Rabbi Hazman paused. "In the early days, all the men who were Rabbis were great men," he explained, and Ruthy smiled with him.

"Well, Hillel was everything a man should be. He

was good and kind and wise and great. He knew, it was said, not only all the wisdom in the Torah, but he knew all the different meanings of the words of the Torah. And one day a brash young man came up to him and said: 'Ho, ho, Rabbi. If you are so smart, tell me what is in that big book, your Torah. Tell me while I stand on one foot.' The young man was sure that nobody could be so smart as to rattle off all the wisdom in the Torah in so short a time.

"But Rabbi Hillel was not at all daunted. 'Never do to others, what is hateful to you,' he said. 'That is the heart of the Torah. All the rest is commentary. Now go and learn.' "

Rabbi Hazman smiled and spread out his hands. "So you see you do not have to be afraid to learn. It is really not so much to know."

Ruthy took a deep breath.

"It's what you do that counts, Ruthy," the Rabbi said softly. "A person sometimes cannot control his thoughts, but he can and should control his actions. Jews believe it's what you do that counts."

Ruthy could not look at him. She wondered if she should tell him about going to the Sunday school party and putting up a Christmas tree for the dog. She glanced at him. He sat there smiling at her.

"Confession is not part of our faith," he said gently. "Judaism recognizes that men are only human — and imperfect. But confession is made only to yourself.

For unless you recognize what you have done wrong, you cannot do what is right."

Ruthy sat back in her chair.

"Heaven," the Rabbi said. "We believe our heaven can be here on earth." He shrugged. "And who knows, some day, maybe, if all men work together, the world will be a heaven to live in. That's what we hope for, Ruthy."

Ruthy sat there thinking and the Rabbi picked up his pen again. She sat waiting, politely, until he looked up. He looked at her questioning.

"You are waiting for something?" he said.

"My lesson," Ruthy reminded him. "I was supposed to come to have a Bas Mitzvah lesson."

The Rabbi smiled. He waved his hand toward the door. "Go," he said. "You have had your lesson. And you will be here next week — " he looked at his calendar — "same time?"

Ruthy nodded and walked out. She stood outside his door a few moments in wonder. It had never occurred to her that she was having a Bas Mitzvah lesson. She thought they had only been talking!

She moved quickly down the hall and out of the building. She sat on the bus going home, thinking about her first lesson. She wasn't quite sure yet just what it was she had learned. Other than a joke. She grinned, and settled back into her seat. Getting ready for her Bas Mitzvah was quite different from what she had expected it to be. It was quite different, indeed.

Herbert was standing there on the corner when she got off the bus. She didn't say anything to him, not even when he swung around and walked beside her.

"It's okay," he said, then, suddenly. "I paid up for you."

She looked at him wondering if he had gone crazy. "You what?"

"That money you and Sandra spent. I paid it back for you." He kicked at a stone and didn't look at her.

Ruthy stopped walking. "What money? I don't owe her any money. What are you talking about?"

He stopped then too, and came back a step or two to face her. "You mean, you don't really know?"

Impatiently she poked him with her elbow. "Don't know what?"

"Look, didn't you and Sandra buy ice cream every day after school for a week?"

"Yes. But Sandra treated. She didn't say anything about paying her back."

"Sandra treated? With what?"

"Her money." Ruthy licked her lips. "At least she said it was her money." And then she remembered, Sandra hadn't said whose money it was at all. All she had said was "mum's the word."

"It wasn't her money," Herbert said. "She took it from her mother's purse. And she told her mother you did it together."

Ruthy gasped. She turned swiftly and ran down the block to Sandra's house.

Sandra was sitting in her bedroom staring out the window. When she saw Ruthy coming, she opened it and stuck her head out. She said, "I've been expecting you, I guess."

Ruthy stood before her, her arms folded. Suddenly she couldn't say any of the things she had intended to say. She saw Sandra had been crying.

"All I told her at first was that we'd done it together," Sandra said. "I didn't mean taking it together, I meant spending it. But my mother didn't know that. She said I couldn't play with you anymore."

Ruthy opened her mouth but she didn't exactly know what to say.

"She knows it now," said Sandra. "I'm supposed to apologize to you. I'm supposed to give Herbert back the money he gave me. I'm supposed to . . ." Sandra gulped for although there were no sobs the tears were rolling down her cheeks.

Ruthy felt in her coat pocket, found a crumpled tissue, and blew her nose. Then she put the tissue back into her pocket again.

"I thought it was your Christmas money," she said.

Sandra hiccupped. "That's what I thought you would think it was," she said. "But my mother didn't think so. Anyway, she made me put my Christmas

money in my bank. So it wasn't exactly stealing."

Ruthy looked at her contemplatively.

Sandra flushed. "Well, maybe it was exactly like stealing. But, anyway, *I* didn't think it was."

Ruthy said, "Your mother did, though."

Sandra grimaced, as if even the memory of what her mother had thought was painful. Then she sighed. "I can't go to a show or to a party for a whole month. When she missed it, she thought at first she had paid the cleaners and forgotten. That's how I got away with it so long."

"You didn't really expect to get away with it forever, did you?" Ruthy asked curiously.

Sandra glanced at her quickly. She said then, in an uncertain tone, "I don't know. I guess I really wasn't thinking much at all." She sniffed loudly. "I have to pay it back out of my allowance."

Ruthy looked at her sympathetically.

"My mother said if you lie and steal when you are young, there's no telling what you'll do when you're grown up."

"I don't really think there's any danger of your growing up to be a bank robber," Ruthy comforted.

Sandra giggled. Then her expression sobered. "I guess I'll be punished when I get to heaven — " she added dourly, "if I get to heaven."

Ruthy smiled to herself. When you were Jewish you didn't believe in that kind of heaven.

"Just a minute," Sandra said, and closed her window.

She came out a moment later, buttoning her coat. "I can play for only a half hour. I told Marguerite I'd go over to her house in half an hour. She's practicing her piano lesson." Sandra put her arm through Ruthy's. "But I don't really have to go," she said.

They walked along together, arm in arm, down the street toward Mrs. Byrd's house. A car was parked at the corner, and a man was sitting in it writing in a notebook.

"A telephone man?" Sandra guessed.

Ruthy peered at the car. It was white and had an insignia on the door. She shook her head. "Looks more like an official to me."

Sandra guessed again. "The mayor?"

"Most likely the Lord High Executioner," Ruthy said. They giggled together.

"Pardon me." The man got out of his car and took off his hat. "I'm from the Humane Society," he said.

Ruthy stood very still.

"I have a complaint here about a couple of cats." He studied the notebook in his hand.

"Oh, that would be Mr. Harvey's cats," Sandra said eagerly.

Ruthy glared at her.

"He lives in the alley," Sandra said. "You go around the house and it's that little house facing the alley."

The man thanked them both and went around the house. Ruthy ran after him.

"You're not going to take Mr. Harvey's cats, are you?" she asked.

He smiled at her anxiety. "I'm not about to take anything. All I'm supposed to do is notify him of a complaint. You the complainee?"

"Me! I should say not. It's Mrs. Byrd. She doesn't like cats. She doesn't like dogs, either."

"That's too bad," the man said as he turned into the alley.

"She can't really do anything, can she?" Ruthy asked.

The man paused. "Well, that depends. If she catches them on her property and calls us, we'd have to pick them up. Or," he looked at Ruthy with his eyebrows raised ominously, "if the complaint is big enough she might have him arrested."

Ruthy stood there and watched him go down the alley and knock on Mr. Harvey's door. He knocked on Mr. Harvey's door and waited. Then he knocked again.

"I guess maybe he's not at home," Ruthy called. She tried not to show her smile.

The man glanced at her briefly, knocked once more, consulted his wrist watch, shrugged, and went back to his car.

Ruthy followed him back to the front street. She looked around. Sandra was not there. For a moment, she reflected, she had forgotten all about Sandra. And then she saw her, marching resolutely up to Marguerite's door.

# 14

RUTHY stood at the kitchen window eating peanut butter and bread. Mrs. Byrd's NO TRESPASSING sign curled in the breeze. She wondered if Mrs. Byrd expected the cats to pay any attention to it.

When Herbert came in, she said to him, "Do you think they have a special section in jail for trespassing cats?"

Herbert glanced out the window to the sign. "She won't call the police, she'll call the Humane Society. The sign makes it more legal. But she's got to catch the cats on her property and keep them there before the Humane Society will come out and pick them up. She can call from morning until night and complain and they won't do a thing unless the cats are trespassing and she catches them at it. Then it's legal for her to catch them and hold them until they come and pick the animals up."

Their grandmother looked at Herbert with loving admiration. "A lawyer," she said. "Herbert already has a head for a lawyer. It's a fine business," she said approvingly.

Herbert looked modest, and added with a new pontifical quality to his tone, "Anyway, it's all bluff. She won't catch them because she's afraid of them. She wouldn't touch them with a ten-foot pole."

Ruthy looked out the window. Mrs. Byrd was shaking her bathroom curtains out of the upstairs window. She seemed to be shaking them into the wind that carried the dust and dirt over the fence onto Mr. Harvey's prized rosebushes. It was Ruthy's personal opinion that Mrs. Byrd wasn't afraid of anything at all. She fixed herself another peanut butter sandwich, and went out into the backyard to eat it.

She stood in the middle of the yard munching at the bread. Across the alley, the cats were sitting on the fence between Mr. Harvey's and Mrs. Byrd's yard. They were sitting on Mr. Harvey's fence. The door to Mr. Harvey's house was closed. Ruthy jumped up onto the first branch of the cherry tree to finish her sandwich.

Suddenly a very strange thing occurred. The two cats, first Eliza and then Bib, jumped down from the fence into Mrs. Byrd's yard, stepped across the grass and walked through Mrs. Byrd's open basement door. Ruthy stared in surprise, and she almost fell out of the tree in amazement when she perceived Mrs. Byrd tiptoe out of her kitchen door, go down the outside steps to her basement door, and bang it shut.

Then she went back into her kitchen quickly. Ruthy slid out of the tree in a hurry. She ran across the alley and knocked briskly on the door to the little house.

"She's got your cats!" Ruthy said breathlessly as

Mr. Harvey opened the door.

Mr. Harvey's eyes seemed icy blue as they stared out at her. Suddenly his face turned red.

"She's got them trapped in her basement," Ruthy told him quickly. "She put some catnip or something they like on the basement steps and left the door open, and now she's got them locked down there and I bet she's calling the Humane Society to come pick them up."

Mr. Harvey turned swiftly and picked up his cane. Without even buttoning his sweater he came out into the cold and strode up the alley, into Mrs. Byrd's backyard.

Mrs. Byrd saw him through the window and came out on her porch. "You're trespassing on my property, Mr. Harvey!" she called out in high warning.

"I'm doing more than that!" Mr. Harvey said and he brandished his cane.

Mrs. Byrd's face grew white and she quickly stepped back into the house and closed the door. Ruthy held her breath.

But Mr. Harvey had no intention of frightening Mrs. Byrd with his cane. He used it instead as a rapier and rammed it against the small basement window. The glass shattered with a tinkling sound, and with a quick sweep of his cane he squared off the hole. Then he grunted hoarsely into the window. The cats jumped out, one after the other. Eliza on Mr. Harvey's shoulder, and Bib limping at his heels,

formed a dignified procession out of the yard.

Mrs. Byrd opened her door wide. "I'll have the police on you!" she shouted. But Mr. Harvey merely turned his head and waved, almost a friendly wave, as he marched into his house.

Mrs. Byrd spied Ruthy standing in the middle of the alley. "You saw that!" she demanded. "You saw what he did, didn't you?"

Ruthy opened her mouth, and felt at the same time a firm hand laid on her shoulder. She turned at the unexpected touch. Her father stood beside her.

"Is there something the matter, Mrs. Byrd?" he called pleasantly. "We heard something, but we weren't sure what. You know we can't see into your yard from ours at all, can we, Ruthy?"

Ruthy searched her father's face. "I guess not," she said reluctantly.

Mrs. Byrd sniffed and closed her door. Ruthy followed her father into their own house. He walked stiffly, almost jerkily, the way he did when he was angry.

Ruthy closed the back door behind her. "Well, I don't care!" she burst out. "I would have told her what I saw. I would have told her I saw her laying a trap for the cats and making them come into her basement — that's what I would have told her."

Her father sat down at the kitchen table. "Shut up, Ruthy," he said, and it was the choice of his words rather than the sound of his anger that made her stare at him in surprise. It was the way she and Herbert talked to each other, not the way her father usually talked to them.

"That's what I mean," he said, "in plain language — language you understand — shut up. Now and from now on!"

Ruthy dropped down into a chair across from him.

"We don't want to quarrel with our neighbors. Do you understand? We are not going to stick our noses into other people's business. They don't bother us; we're not going to bother them."

"But — " said Ruthy.

"Not but's!" said her father. "No if's, no and's, and no but's!"

Ruthy clamped her lips closed and stared out the window.

"We've always been careful to get along with our neighbors," her father said.

Ruthy only pressed her lips more firmly together. *Careful!* It was a word too familiar to her ears. All her life they had lived *careful.*

"Be careful not to bother the neighbors," she and Herbert had been admonished every time they had been sent outside to play. Her father had always been careful to keep the lawn mowed as regularly as the neighbors' mowed theirs. Her mother was careful to wash out the garbage can regularly, and not to stand on the back step and shout after them. She and Herbert had to be careful to keep the garage door closed so that the neighbors would not be offended by the sight of the clutter of the necessary tools and cartons kept stacked neatly on the back wall. When the newsboys let some of the papers drop and fly, it was her grandmother who was careful to retrieve the flying sheets. "It's a shame for the neighbors," she would explain as she rolled them together and put them into the trash can.

Ruthy stared out the window at Mrs. Byrd's house. She had never seen Mrs. Byrd worrying about being careful for *them* or anybody else.

"What if she calls the police and puts Mr. Harvey in jail?" Ruthy heard herself shout.

Strangely, her father smiled. "She's not going to call the police about this," he said. "The only one she's going to call is the fix-it shop to come and repair the window. She knows it and Mr. Harvey knows it and we know it."

Nevertheless, Mrs. Byrd was going to try again to get rid of Mr. Harvey's cats, thought Ruthy. She knew it; and she knew Mrs. Byrd knew it, and she wondered that her father didn't know it, too.

# 15

RUTHY sat at the kitchen table, studying the portion she would read from the Torah on her Bas Mitzvah, as she tasted the cookies her grandmother was busy baking for the event.

"They're good!" she said, noting her grandmother's frown as she helped herself to another.

"And why shouldn't they be good?" her grandmother said bitterly.

Ruthy raised her eyes from her book to regard her grandmother. "What's the matter?"

"What should be the matter?" her grandmother replied with a thrust of her shoulders.

Ruthy put her finger in her place in the book and waited.

"Etta Kaplan!" burst out her grandmother. "Do you know what she says? A Bas Mitzvah without chopped liver and herring is not a Bas Mitzvah at all, she says! She says to serve only a little cookies and maybe cake to her is skimpy. Hah! Skimpy. One hundred and fifty dozen cookies I will have ready and she calls it skimpy! Do you know what?"

Ruthy shook her head.

"I think she is talking because she is mad. And she is mad because I didn't ask her to make herring for the

Bas Mitzvah." Her grandmother clasped her hands before her with a resounding smack. "Because I did not ask her to make herring for your Bas Mitzvah, she is mad!"

Ruthy smiled. She didn't like herring particularly. But what she did like was everyone getting all excited about preparations for her Bas Mitzvah. It was the month of March, only two weeks before her Bas Mitzvah.

"I should think she'd be pleased to be saved all that work," Ruthy said.

Her grandmother looked at her with exasperation. "Work? It's not the work she's worried about. It's the honor."

"Honor?" Ruthy couldn't see any particular honor connected with making herring. "What do you mean honor?"

Her grandmother sat down for a minute. "A Bas Mitzvah is a mitzvah, don't you see?"

Ruthy shook her head.

"A mitzvah is a good deed, a thing that is good in itself. It is its own reward. To take part in a mitzvah — to have something to do with it — is a special honor. So — " her grandmother spread out her hands — "because we did not invite her to make her herring for your Bas Mitzvah, she feels slighted, not honored."

Ruthy sighed. It all seemed very complicated to her.

Her mother came into the kitchen, just in time to hear the last words.

"Etta, I suppose," she said. She smiled.

Her grandmother shrugged. "Who else but Etta." She said complacently, "But you have to admit, she has a heart of gold." The grandmother sighed. "Do you think maybe I should ask her to bake her strudel?"

Mrs. Morgen grinned. "I asked her already. I met her down at the supermarket. She had already filled her basket with oil and nuts and a couple of packages of raisins, but I pretended not to see them and asked her as if I wasn't sure she would honor us by accepting."

The picture rose to Ruthy's mind, of Etta with her loaded cart waiting to be asked to bake her strudel. She laughed, catching her mother's eye. "Oh, I like her," she said quickly. "Honestly, I'm really beginning to like her."

"Who?" asked Herbert. He came through the kitchen door and left it open behind him. His grandmother frowned.

"Close the door," she said. "You want Ruthy to catch cold right before her Bas Mitzvah?"

Ruthy swallowed her smile as Herbert went back and closed the door. She remembered how it was when all the concern of their grandmother was on him. She looked at him wondering if he remembered it too. But his mind seemed to be on something else.

"Mrs. Byrd is out there yelling at Mr. Harvey's cats again," he remarked as he swiped a cooky from the plate on the table. His grandmother lightly slapped at his hand, and then she gave him two cookies more.

Ruthy looked out the window with interest. It had rained almost every day throughout the last two months. The rain had streaked the cardboard No Trespassing sign and softened its edges.

"Where's Mr. Harvey?" Ruthy tried to see whether he was out there, too.

Herbert helped himself to another cooky. "Inside his house, I guess. There are two men there, spreading fertilizer over his garden. They brought a whole truckful. Sandra's mother bought some too. Just a little sack of it — " he grinned — "for her dahlias. She asked me to carry it around the house for her so she wouldn't get her gloves dirty."

"What were you doing over at Sandra's?" Ruthy asked.

"I didn't say I was over at Sandra's," he said.

"Well, where were you then?"

"Over at Marguerite's," Herbert said with a grin, and walked out.

Hastily Ruthy put on her scarf and coat. She opened the kitchen door. "I'm going over to Sandra's house," she yelled over her shoulder, and ran out.

"Anything new?" Sandra asked listlessly as the girls sat on the davenport in her front window. They could see right out to the front street, right over to Marguerite's front yard, too. Sandra must have been sitting there looking out for some time.

"My Bas Mitzvah is in two weeks," Ruthy answered, but she wasn't thinking about her Bas Mitzvah. She was thinking about Marguerite and Herbert.

Evidently Sandra was thinking about the same thing too.

"*He* was over there all morning!" she said suddenly, vehemently. "Imagine! All morning long. Honestly! My mother wouldn't let me sit around talking to a boy practically all day like that."

Ruthy tried to be sympathetically helpful. "Well, as you once said, 'that's Marguerite!' "

"And you know something else?" Sandra turned around to face her squarely.

Somehow Ruthy knew that whatever Sandra was going to say was what bothered her most. Ruthy shook her head.

"After your brother left, guess what?"

"What?"

"*Another* boy came over. He came right over. I've never even seen him before!"

Ruthy said, "Look, why don't we walk around the block instead of just sitting here." In full view of Marguerite and her visitors, she meant. "It's nice out. Almost spring."

"All right." Sandra sighed as she tied a scarf under her chin.

They walked down the street passing Mr. Harvey's

fenced-in yard which was really his backyard, though it faced the street, and they paused a moment in front of Mrs. Byrd's house.

"Don't step on the grass," Sandra mimicked, and giggled.

Ruthy put one foot experimentally on the plushy strip of green. "I just want to see if the green comes off," she said. She pulled her foot back quickly as Mrs. Byrd's front door opened.

Mrs. Byrd threw them a sharp look and then she

smiled. A mincing smile, thought Ruthy.

"Hello there, girls," Mrs. Byrd called to them.

She was all dressed up, Ruthy noted. She had a fur collar around her neck. Over her arm hung her black leather purse by its strap, and in her hands was a large rolled up paper. She waved it at them.

"Are your mothers home?" she asked as she came down the steps.

"My mother isn't," Sandra said. "She's downtown."

"Well, I'll start at your house, then," she said to Ruthy, and passing them, turned the corner toward the Morgens' house.

The two girls looked at each other.

"If she's collecting for anything but United Good Neighbors, she'd better not come to our house," Sandra said. "My mother said there are too many people asking for charity these days."

"I wonder if she's going to Mr. Harvey's house," Ruthy reflected out loud.

"You know what she did yesterday, don't you? She was around talking about a petition. She told my mother she was going to get the whole neighborhood to sign a petition saying the cats are a public nuisance. Mrs. Byrd told my mother it was everyone's duty to sign it."

"Do you mean to say that if everyone signs a petition they can come and take away Mr. Harvey's cats!"

"Sure," said Sandra. "Why not?"

Ruthy thought of Mr. Harvey nestling the cat under his rough chin. "But they're his cats!" she said.

Sandra shrugged . . . "They're just alley cats. They're not worth much."

Ruthy heard her voice getting louder. "Not to you, maybe. But they're worth something to Mr. Harvey. They're worth a lot!"

Sandra looked at her with a funny expression. "What do you care about Mr. Harvey? It isn't as if he is anybody. Why my mother said that in some neighborhoods they wouldn't even stand for his living there. She says this is a residential district and there should be a law against people raising chickens and potatoes on a city lot."

"He doesn't raise chickens!" Ruthy said with anger.

Daintily Sandra pinched the tip of her nose with two fingers. "Phew," she said. "It always smells like he does."

"That's not chickens, that's fertilizer. It doesn't smell any worse on Mr. Harvey's potatoes than it does on your mother's dahlias!"

"It does if it's Mr. Harvey's," Sandra said breezily. "Everything about his place smells bad — including him, his garden and his dirty old cats." She turned about abruptly and walked away.

Ruthy shouted after her. "He doesn't smell any worse than you do!"

But Sandra pretended not to hear her, and turned in at Marguerite's house.

Ruthy ran home. She entered the kitchen just as

she heard the front doorbell. "Don't let her in!" she shouted to whoever might be in the living room nearer the door. "Pretend like no one's home and don't let her in!"

She dashed through the house into the living room —and stopped. Mrs. Byrd was sitting on the davenport with the white paper unrolled on her lap.

# 16

MRS. MORGEN gave Ruthy an odd look. "You might as well answer the door," she said.

Ruthy moved quickly into the front hall. A man in a black coat was standing there on the front porch. He wore no hat, and his coat collar was turned up to warm his ears. He held a little brown leather satchel. He nodded when Ruthy opened the door.

"I've been clear around this whole block twice," he said, "and I can't seem to put my finger on this address." He consulted a little card he held in his hand. "I'm looking for Harvey, Eleazar Harvey."

Hastily Ruthy stepped out and closed the door behind her. "You're not from the Humane Society are you? Or the police station?"

He laughed, an odd sort of cackle. "Not exactly. I'm a doctor."

"You didn't come about the cats?" Ruthy asked, her voice sounding anxious.

"I don't think so," the doctor said. "Unless Eleazar Harvey is . . ." He grinned.

Ruthy grinned too. "That's all right then," she said. "Mr. Harvey lives in the little house on the alley. That's why you couldn't find it. You have to go through the alley to get to his front door. I'll walk around with you," she offered. "It's closer if you just cut through our backyard and use our back gate."

The doctor followed her around the house. "Rather odd, isn't it, for a house to face the alley instead of the street?"

Ruthy said firmly, "There's nothing odd about Mr. Harvey at all. He just likes to live alone. And he's got two cats."

"Well, I guess that's odd enough for some people," the doctor said, but the way he smiled, Ruthy knew he didn't mean himself. "Fact is," the doctor said as Ruthy opened the back gate, "in my business, I see more who are odd than who aren't. Sometimes I wonder if there is anyone *even* at all, if you know what I mean?"

Ruthy laughed. "You have to knock pretty hard on his door," she said. "He has no doorbell, and that little hole at the bottom is a cat hole. His cats go in and out as they please."

"How very neat," the doctor said, and rapped loudly on the door.

Inside the cats began to mew, but there was no other sound. The doctor rapped again.

"That's funny," said Ruthy. "He's almost always home."

"I suspect he's in bed," the doctor said. "That's what the message said. "Why don't I just try the door — " he did and the doorknob turned easily — "and go right in." He paused on the threshold. "Hello-o, Mr. Harvey!" he called.

There was a hoarse sound from inside. The doctor stepped in and closed the door behind him.

Ruthy sat down on Mr. Harvey's porch step and waited. She wondered if Mr. Harvey was sick — very sick, that is. The two cats pushed at their own door and stepped gracefully out. They sat with her on the step until the door opened. Ruthy jumped up.

The doctor came out. He smiled at her. He didn't look worried or anything. He only looked interested.

"I'm going to cut through your yard again, if I may," he said, "and drive my car around."

"That's all right," Ruthy said.

"I'm going to take Mr. Harvey to the hospital for a few days. Nasty throat he has."

"What about his cats?" Ruthy asked. "I don't think Mr. Harvey will want to go anywhere without his cats."

The doctor paused. "That's funny," he said. "That's exactly what he said." And then he stopped smiling. "But I really think he has to go to the hospital without his cats."

The door flew open. Mr. Harvey stood there, a scarf around his neck, and an old flannel bathrobe tied tightly around him.

"I don't need to go to any hospital, I tell you." Then he grew red with coughing. The doctor and

Ruthy looked at each other.

"You won't have to worry about your cats, Mr. Harvey," Ruthy said. "I'll feed them every day. I'll put their food on the porch just as you do, and you can lock the door and they can go in and out through their own door by themselves just as they always do."

The doctor smiled. "Fine," he said.

Mr. Harvey didn't say anything more. He went back into the house and put on his shoes.

"Now don't you worry about a thing!" Ruthy called after him as the doctor helped him into the car. "You can depend on me," she said. "I'll take good care of your cats."

Mr. Harvey lifted his hand weakly to wave as the car eased out of the alley and turned the corner. It was then Ruthy remembered about Mrs. Byrd and her petition.

She hurried into her house. "You didn't sign anything, did you?"

Her mother looked at her with impatience. "Ruthy, what are you talking about?"

"About Mrs. Byrd's petition. She's trying to get rid of Mr. Harvey's cats again."

Her mother picked up a needle and threaded it expertly. "She didn't say anything about a petition."

Herbert said, "But she did say something about the cats. She said that she has registered another complaint and they promised to send another man out to talk to Mr. Harvey and she said if he doesn't get rid of them then, she will."

"How?" Ruthy asked. She had a vision of Mr. Harvey being taken from the hospital to the jail.

"It's not nice for neighbors to fight," her grandmother said, bustling in and out of the room. "The old man should stay on his side of the fence and Mrs. Byrd should stay on hers. That's what fences were made for."

Mrs. Morgen said, "Mrs. Byrd was showing me the new plan for the Community Church building. They want everyone in the neighborhood to contribute."

"You mean give them money to build a new church?"

"Why not?" said Mr. Morgen. He had just come in, and stood there, taking off his coat. "She's a do-gooder, Mrs. Byrd is." He hung up his coat.

"Very civic minded," Mrs. Morgen agreed.

Ruthy snorted . . . "She's not much of a do-gooder to Mr. Harvey."

"Her arguments with her neighbor are her own private business," Ruthy's father said mildly. "I daresay Mr. Harvey can take care of himself."

"No, he can't," Ruthy said. "Not right now anyway. He's sick. The doctor took him to the hospital."

"Tch, tch." Clicking sympathetically her grandmother came to the table and sat down. "A man alone like that."

"He's not alone," Ruthy said. "He's got his cats."

"You mean they let him take his cats to the hospital?" Herbert asked, as if he thought that was funny.

Ruthy made a face at him. "Of course not," she said. "He left the cats home."

"He left the cats home by themselves?" Her grandmother looked shocked.

Ruthy shook her head. "He left them home with me."

For a few seconds Ruthy heard the clock ticking in the silence of the kitchen.

"With you?" her father repeated as if he hadn't heard her right.

"What has it to do with you?" her mother said.

"You shouldn't mix into things that don't concern you," her grandmother scolded. "It has nothing to do with you."

"It does too. It has something to do with everybody!" Ruthy could see they thought she wasn't making much sense.

"I promised," she said trying to explain.

"Then he was wrong to ask you," her grandmother said. "He shouldn't have asked you to take care of anything."

Furiously Ruthy turned upon all of them. "He didn't ask me!" she shouted. "He didn't ask me anything at all!"

# 17

RUTHY sat dejectedly in the chair before the Rabbi's desk, only half listening to his explanation of the meaning of the Torah portion she would read on her Bas Mitzvah day. "A promise is a promise," Ruthy whispered to herself.

The Rabbi paused and sat looking at her.

"You have studied the portion I gave you."

She nodded.

"You know the special prayers by heart." He named and counted off the requirements. "You can read from the Torah in Hebrew, and translate what you read. You know the meaning of what you translate. You will do very well," he said firmly.

Ruthy sighed, and tried to put her mind on his words. But it wouldn't stay there. She stared at the book lying open on the desk. It was the story of Hanukah. How the king ordered all Jews to bow down to idols. Only they wouldn't. Not even when they were put to death for refusing. Ruthy guessed it had never been easy to be a Jew.

"I can't see why those people chose to stay Jewish," she said idly.

The Rabbi slapped his knee with his hand. "Choose?" he said with surprise. "What has it to do with choice? You don't choose your religion; you are part of it. How you think and how you act and what you believe and how you live. You!"

Thoughtfully Ruthy looked at the book again. "When am I supposed to tell you what my Bas Mitzvah means to me?" she asked.

"It's not important that you tell me, Ruthy," Rabbi Hazeman said.

She looked at him surprised.

"It is only for yourself that you must know. As why I am a Rabbi is only for myself."

She looked away remembering the presumptuous question she had asked him that first day of her lessons.

"There are some things you must know for sure in your heart," he said. "But for yourself. Only for yourself."

Ruthy looked past him, over his shoulder. "Suppose you were doing something that everybody thought was wrong. And you know it's right," she said.

"You're asking me?" the Rabbi said.

Ruthy nodded. Thoughtfully the Rabbi regarded her. He didn't answer for a long time. At last he said, "To someone else, I might answer something different. But to you, Ruthy, I will say — you do what you have to do. That's all you can do — what you have to."

Ruthy sat up. She closed her book although the lesson time was only half over. "Thank you," she said, standing up. "Thank you very much." And she went out of the room and carefully closed the door.

At her corner, she jumped off the bus and ran the last block home. But she didn't go immediately into the house. She went around through the backyard and across the alley. She had barricaded the little cat hole in Mr. Harvey's door so that the cats would be safe inside. Now she removed the bricks she had piled up there to keep the door from being pushed open.

The cats came out, and sat on the porch step and washed themselves and looked aggrieved. Ruthy grinned. For some strange reason they reminded her of Mrs. Kaplan and her daughter Etta, and she laughed out loud.

She let them exercise a few moments then she put them back inside Mr. Harvey's house and barricaded the door again.

Ruthy slowly walked across the alley through her backyard and into the kitchen of her house.

"Hi," she said.

Her grandmother, busy at the stove, looked at her and then away again. There was an odd look on her grandmother's face. A look of pain, or maybe it was withheld indignation. Ruthy felt a hollowness inside her. She wondered if her grandmother had decided not to speak to her anymore.

"Ruthy, set the table," her mother said, and Ruthy looked quickly at her too. Her mother's voice sounded strange, stranger than it had ever sounded before.

"What's the matter?" she said.

Herbert came in at that moment. He answered for them. "It's Prince," he said. And Ruthy looked at him in surprise. Herbert had been crying.

"What's the matter with Prince?"

"Someone poisoned him, that's what's the matter!" Herbert wiped his sleeve over his newly moist eyes.

Mrs Morgen said sharply, "We don't really know that. All we know is that he ate something that poisoned him."

"Where is he? Is he all right?"

"Dad took him to the dog hospital," Herbert said. "The vet is keeping him there overnight. They *think* he's going to be all right."

Ruthy placed the mats on the kitchen table. Her father came into the kitchen and opened the refrigerator. "He's all right," he said. There was a trace of anger in his voice. He closed the refrigerator door without even looking inside, and sat down at the kitchen table.

For a moment he sat there, his elbows on the table, his head in his hands. Ruthy remembered how her grandmother had once musingly told her that her father would have made an ideal butcher.

"A butcher!" she had cried in surprise.

"A butcher of kosher meats," her grandmother had explained with a whimsical smile.

Meats labeled "kosher," Ruthy knew, had to come from animals slaughtered in a certain way. But her father a butcher! It was impossible to imagine.

"A kosher butcher," her grandmother had told her, "must be a gentle man. For a gentle man will keep his long knife thin and very sharp with no nicks. According to Jewish law, animals must be killed quickly and surely and cleanly. Death must come without suffering." Her grandmother had nodded over her story, smiling. "Yes, your father would be the best of all butchers. He cannot bear to see anyone suffer — not even an animal."

Ruthy had never known what her grandmother had meant. Seeing her father now, his head in his hands, suddenly she understood.

Her father raised his head to look at her. "The cats?"

Ruthy nodded. "They're all right."

Ruthy finished setting the table. There was a lump in her throat when she sat down with the others.

She picked up a fork and heard it clatter to the floor as she started suddenly. "Do you mean someone tried to poison the cats, too?"

Herbert laughed hollowly. "Not too," he said. "Instead of. Someone put two pieces of poisoned fish on Mr. Harvey's garbage can lid. Crazy Prince knocked the lid off. Good thing he doesn't like fish much. He tasted just enough to make him throw up like crazy."

Ruthy looked out the window at the NO TRESPASSING sign on Mrs. Byrd's gate, and then she looked quickly at her father.

He shook his head. "It could have been an accident," he said gently. And then he straightened his shoulders and raised his head. "It *was* an accident," he said firmly. "And Prince will be all right."

Ruthy pressed her lips together.

"Well, I can tell you, I wish the old man was home from the hospital already," her grandmother said.

Ruthy looked around the table. It was plain to see that it was what her father wished, and her mother, and Herbert too. And, all of a sudden, she wished it too.

# 18

DURING the next few days, Ruthy did her best to keep the cats safe for Mr. Harvey. She let them out every morning before school, and stayed there, sitting on Mr. Harvey's porch step with her coat buttoned up tight and her scarf around her ears, keeping an eye on them.

She checked the garbage can covers every day to see they were tight, and fed the animals only when she was there to watch them eat. They seemed to be happy enough to go back into Mr. Harvey's house and wait for him. Eliza especially seemed to miss him. She was happiest when Ruthy sat on the step and held her close to her chin, while Bib was content to sit on her foot. Dutifully they ate what she set before them each day, and washed their faces and scolded each other regularly.

Prince came home weak, but his appetite picked up quickly. He didn't like cats; making no bones about it, they didn't like him.

"When Mr. Harvey gets home, he'll let you out more," she promised Bib. And to Eliza she whispered, "You just wait until Mr. Harvey comes home. Everything will be all right for you then. You'll see."

She was pleased to see that they trusted her, and

she ran home from school every day wondering whether Mr. Harvey might have come back while she was at school.

They didn't talk about it anymore in front of her. Not her brother who kept watching her curiously, nor her grandmother whose wrinkled frown seemed to be permanently etched on her face as she mixed and rolled and baked the final batches of cookies for the Bas Mitzvah.

Her father tried to explain how it was. He talked about learning to live with the people around them. He talked about facing reality. By reality he meant Mrs. Byrd. And while he talked, Ruthy thought of Mr. Harvey and his little family of cats. She thought of Mr. Harvey not going to the hospital until he had known his cats would be taken care of. He hadn't expected to stay so long. He had expected to come home in a short time to them and his roses. A tear rolled from one of the inner corners of Ruthy's eyes down her nose. Quickly she wiped it away.

Awkwardly her father patted her shoulder. "I knew you'd understand," he said. There was relief in his voice.

Ruthy nodded. She understood all right. She understood that her father wouldn't let her keep the cats much longer.

She sat on Mr. Harvey's step and watched the cats daintily pick their way through the alley. Bib jumped to the top of the fence and looked over into Mrs. Byrd's yard.

"Come back!" Ruthy said severely. "You've got to stay here or Mrs. Byrd might poison you again." The cat jumped down and came over to sit on Ruthy's foot.

Her mother said bluntly, "What you should be thinking about is your Bas Mitzvah, not the cats."

"But I am thinking about my Bas Mitzvah!" Ruthy said loudly.

Her mother looked at her with a strange expression. Ruthy sighed. Her feelings about Mr. Harvey, the cats, and her Bas Mitzvah — they were all inextricably bound together. Yet she could not explain why.

Sitting on Mr. Harvey's step watching the cats, she gave some thought to it. It was strange, she reflected, she had really never known Mr. Harvey well. You might say she had not known him at all until the day Prince had jumped on his cats. She remembered Sandra saying he smelled. She remembered how she had jumped to his defense almost as if it were she Sandra was making fun of. She had acted as if the problem was not Mr. Harvey's but her own. Ruthy shook herself a little and frowned.

Mrs. Byrd came out on to her back porch with a broom. She began to sweep her steps.

"Come on cats!" Ruthy called, and led the way into her yard.

They followed her willingly. But Prince was there.

He stretched his front paws out before him and made a little jump in the direction of the cats. He growled.

"Stop that!" Ruthy said crossly, thrusting him away.

He paid no attention.

She glared at him. "They've got as much right to live as you have." She listened to the sound of her own words.

The dog only growled louder.

"Stop that!" she shouted at him and hardly knew why she was shouting.

Mrs. Byrd stopped her sweeping and looked over at her.

"Are those nasty cats bothering you?" she called sweetly.

Ruthy turned to look at her. Mrs. Byrd wore a blue flowered apron under her sweater. Her eyebrows were freshly plucked and her hair newly done. But for a second, Ruthy didn't see the smiling face. She saw only a misty blob, which she struggled to see past.

"Everyone has a right to live!" she shouted, only dimly seeing Mrs. Byrd's startled expression. "It's no crime to be different!"

Mrs. Byrd only stood there staring at her and Mrs. Morgen called from an upstairs window.

"Ruthy?" her mother said, a note of questioning in her voice.

Ruthy whirled. She grabbed up the cats, put them back into Mr. Harvey's house, and ran up to her room.

# 19

"Does it make sense to you not to like cats?" she asked Rabbi Hazeman as he ushered her into the sanctuary on the afternoon of her Bas Mitzvah. He was intent on showing her where she would sit, and how she would stand when the Torah was taken from the Ark that evening at the ceremony.

Rabbi Hazeman didn't seem to hear her. He stood before the Ark, the *yarmulka* perched on the back of his head. He touched the velvet curtains which covered the Ark opening, and lifting the corner of the cloth brought it to his lips in a reverent kiss. Curiously, Ruthy watched him.

"It is very old, this Torah," he said, and lifted it from its niche.

It wore a velvet dress with gold embroidered designs. Carefully he removed the silver chain from which dangled a pointer in the shape of a hand with an extended finger. Next he removed an ornate shield, then the velvet wrapper.

Standing at his elbow, Ruthy watched him unroll the scroll of wisdom. Every Sabbath at the regular prayer services a part was read from this book, and because it was her Bas Mitzvah, she, Ruthy, would read the portion for that day.

Ruthy took a deep breath. She read aloud the Hebrew words as the Rabbi pointed them out to her. They echoed strangely in the empty sanctuary. She stumbled, not because of any difficulty in reading the ancient letters, but because it struck her all at once that the words she read had been intoned solemnly by thousands of Jewish people before her. The prayers she would recite were the same prayers her father and her grandfather and the grandfathers before him had recited. The selfsame words.

Ruthy read them out more strongly: "And He shall turn the heart of the fathers to the children, and the heart of the children to their fathers."

Silently she watched the Rabbi gently reroll the scroll at the close of the practice reading.

"Do you know how old you are, Ruthy?" the Rabbi asked as he eased the velvet dress back over the scroll.

Ruthy looked at him with surprise. He knew as well as she did how old she was. A Bar Mitzvah was always held at the age of thirteen.

But he shook his head at her gently. "Today, Ruth," he said, "today on your Bas Mitzvah, you are three thousand years old."

Ruthy blinked.

"Three thousand years ago, Moses brought down from the holy mountain the Ten Commandments." He pointed to a design of the tablets set above the Ark. There they were — the ten rules set down in

Hebrew script. "Bas Mitzvah. Daughter of a Commandment," the Rabbi said.

Bas or bat meant daughter, Ruthy knew. And mitzvah was a Hebrew word for a thing which was good in itself — a commandment.

"Today marks the day you are old enough to recognize the responsibility of your religion: To act justly, to love mercy, and to keep for your good the commandments of the Lord."

Ruthy clasped her hands tightly together. "That's why I have to be responsible for the cats," she said earnestly.

"Eh?" said the Rabbi. But he did not really hear her. He stood gazing at the Torah which he had placed in the open Ark.

He said, as if talking to himself, "To a Jew there are no endings. There are only beginnings." He looked up at the tablets above the Ark. "Perhaps that is the real secret," he said.

"Secret?" said Ruthy. She wondered what the Rabbi was talking about.

He nodded. "Secret of why the people called Jews did not disappear long ago." He gazed at Ruthy intently. "You know what I think?"

Ruthy shook her head.

"I think perhaps it is because the Jews won't bow down to endings — just as they wouldn't bow down to idols. Jews always seem to turn endings into new beginnings. And — who knows" — he rolled his shoulders and smiled at her, "maybe that is why Jews are still here in the world today." He pulled the curtains of the Ark closed.

The final rehearsal was over. Ruthy started down the aisle. She had to feed the cats, she reflected, and take them out a bit before getting ready for her Bas Mitzvah.

"Don't forget to come tonight in plenty of time!" Rabbi Hazeman called after her as she hurried out of the synagogue.

Herbert was there, waiting at the street corner, the way he had been once before. She jumped off the bus step in a hurry, worrying.

"Are they all right?" she asked, wondering whether Mrs. Byrd had tried to poison them again.

Herbert scowled at her. "They're all right," he said.

She walked along beside him a step or two. "Well?"

"Mr. Harvey's not coming back," he said.

Ruthy stopped walking.

"His sister is there now, packing up all his belongings. She says he's her only brother and someone's got to take care of him, and she guesses she's elected."

Ruthy took a deep breath. "Anyway that takes care of the cats," she said. She shook her shoulders conscious of an immense feeling of relief.

Herbert screwed up his face. "Not exactly," he said.

"What do you mean by that?" She started walking again.

He glanced at her and she felt the wariness of his look.

"She says she's not taking the cats. She says she'll have enough to do looking out for a sick man without the trouble of the cats too."

Ruthy broke into a run. Reaching her house, she dashed through the backyard and into the alley. Mr. Harvey was there sitting in his big rocking chair. The chair stood in the middle of the alley, and behind it was a little old pickup truck. A fat woman in jeans was bustling back and forth from the house to the truck. The truck was already full.

The cats, both of them, sat on Mr. Harvey's lap. A blanket was snug around him, and an old woolen cap was pulled down over his ears. But the face that looked out above the blanket and below the cap was gray where it used to be pink.

"Hello," she said breathlessly.

He raised his head to look at her. "I've been waiting for you," he said simply, and the white bristles on his chin quivered in the sharp sunlight.

She nodded, finding it hard to look at the light blue eyes gazing at her so intently. She looked instead at his hands. His wrists were thin, and his fingers moved from one cat to the other as if he could not touch them enough.

Ruthy swallowed.

"They look fine," he said. "They look healthy and fine."

"They missed you," Ruthy said, and suddenly she had to swallow again.

He nodded, and made a loud sound as he cleared his throat.

"You can just shoo them off your lap," the woman in jeans said as she came out of the house again with another armful of stuff. "Like I been telling you. There's not room in my house for those cats."

Mr. Harvey acted as if he didn't hear her.

"There's no call for you to be behaving childishly over them cats," she said with asperity. "We'll just drop them on the road somewhere and they'll get along fine by themselves."

Mr. Harvey jerked violently.

Involuntarily Ruthy took a step toward him. "You don't have to worry about them, Mr. Harvey," she said quickly. She was suddenly conscious of Herbert's face staring at her in surprise over the back fence.

"I'll find a good home for them," she said in a rush of words. "You just see if I don't. I'll find someone who'll take care of them till you get back."

Mr. Harvey's sister snorted. "Get back?" she said. "He'll be lucky if he lives to blueberry-picking time."

But Mr. Harvey smiled at Ruthy over the cats' heads.

"Of course I'll be back," he said. He picked up

Eliza and held the animal out to Ruthy, and gently placed Bib at her feet. Then he twitched the blanket back, unsteadily got to his feet and moved slowly with the help of his cane to the front seat of the truck. His sister helped him to climb in, and then she picked up the rocking chair and put it upside down on top of the load of stuff behind.

"I'll be back," Mr. Harvey said again hoarsely, nodding his thanks at her from the window.

His sister climbed in behind the wheel and started the engine.

"Of course," Ruthy echoed, but it wasn't very loud. Not loud enough even for Mr. Harvey to hear. Ruthy blinked her eyes rapidly and swallowed with all her might.

As the car turned into the street, Mrs. Byrd came out of her house and walked slowly across her yard. She had been standing in her open doorway, listening, all the time.

Bib whined against Ruthy's foot. Ruthy turned to take the cats back into her yard. She wondered suddenly what her father would say to bringing the cats back again. Mrs. Byrd came on towards her. She braced herself for what Mrs. Byrd would say.

"Ruthy." Mrs. Byrd's voice hesitantly reached her.

Ruthy turned.

Mrs. Byrd seemed embarrassed. There were red spots on her neck. It occurred to Ruthy then that some people blush only on their necks. It was a strange thought.

Mrs. Byrd went on with a little rush. "I know you're going to be busy this evening with your Bar Mitzvah and all — "

"*Bas* Mitzvah," Ruthy corrected automatically. But Mrs. Byrd was too intent on her own words to pay any attention.

"And what with your whole family away at church and all . . ."

"Synagogue," Ruthy said softly.

"And it occurred to me that it might be a help to you all if I kept the cats in my basement for you this evening."

"In *your* basement, Mrs. Byrd?" Ruthy's voice rose in surprise.

Mrs. Byrd nodded. She looked off in the direction in which the truck had gone. "After all, seeing as how Mr. Harvey was a neighbor and all, and being so sick — well I feel — under the circumstances — it is only a Christian thing to do." And then she put her hand up to her mouth and looked at Ruthy in consternation. "Oh!" she said. "I didn't mean — "

"That's all right," Ruthy said. "I guess I know what you mean."

# 20

SHE put the cats in Mrs. Byrd's basement and walked slowly home. As she opened the back door the lump in her throat seemed to grow bigger. She went through the kitchen into the dining room. Her father was home early, she saw, and the table was already set for the Friday night dinner.

"We're having dinner a little early tonight," her grandmother said, placing the heavy brass candlesticks on the table.

Ruthy nodded. On Friday nights, Mrs. Morgen used her best dishes and the linen napkins. Tonight there were flowers on the table as well, and the very best wineglasses.

Ruthy didn't say anything when they all sat down at the table. She didn't even join in when her grandmother lighted the Sabbath candles and said the prayer. Feeling Herbert's curious glance on her, she kept her own gaze on her plate. He would tell them, she guessed. He would wait until they finished the soup, and then he would tell them that she had done it again. Suddenly she couldn't seem to swallow another mouthful. She laid her soupspoon down.

"Something the matter with the soup?" her grandmother peered at her.

"I'm not hungry," Ruthy mumbled.

"Not hungry!" her father boomed. "How can anyone sit down to chicken soup and not be hungry?"

Her grandmother motioned him to be quiet. "Maybe a little roast chicken?" She held out the platter enticingly. "A little piece of white meat, or a sliver of noodle pudding?"

Her grandmother's anxious face hovered over her. Her father had stopped eating to look at her. Herbert took a swallow of water and then opened his mouth. He would tell them now, Ruthy knew. He would tell them how she had mixed in again.

"I'm not hungry," said Ruthy louder. And suddenly the constriction in her throat seemed to engulf her. Feeling the tears beginning down her face, Ruthy hastily pushed back her chair. She swallowed the sob, and ran up the stairs to her room.

"It's the excitement," she heard her mother say. "She's a bundle of nerves. Girls always get upset at times like this."

Her father's fond laugh reached her. "It's the Bas Mitzvah," he said. "She's all excited about her Bas Mitzvah."

Ruthy closed her bedroom door. She had almost forgotten about her Bas Mitzvah. That's why her father had come home early, and why the table was set with such care. It was on account of her Bas Mitzvah! Ruthy wiped her face with her arm. She sniffed, and thought about her Bas Mitzvah.

Opening the closet door, she looked at the blue dress hanging there. With her toes she touched the toes of her long white shoes. Tonight she would stand up before the congregation and read from the Torah. She would say the ancient words from that ancient book. She would receive the Rabbi's blessing and walk down the aisle into the reception hall. There she would stand with her parents and receive the congratulations of the members of the congregation. Some of them would give her gifts to mark the occasion. And Sandra and Marguerite would be there. Herbert had arranged to escort them both.

Thoughtfully Ruthy laid the dress on her bed. On the bureau were the gifts that had arrived from the aunts that day. Absently she opened them. A pair of nylon stockings, a calendar set in a silver frame with the days of the Jewish holidays marked in red. A star of David on a chain to wear around her neck. A box of stationery.

Ruthy stared at herself in the mirror. Without special interest, she regarded her "Jewish" nose. It was *her* nose, she thought, as much a part of her face as her feelings were a part of herself. She knew exactly how she felt about certain things. They were as clear to her as the nose on her face.

She looked down at the box of stationery. Then she opened it and pulled out a sheet. TWO WONDERFUL CATS AVAILABLE, she wrote across the top of the paper.

She paused and stared into the mirror without seeing herself. Then she wrote —

> *Must find respectable home for cherished companions. Female is blind in one eye, wonderful temperament. Male has slight limp. Send details on your home to Ruthy Morgen, 3618 Vine Street. Will contact you for interview.*

Ruthy addressed the envelope to the classified department of the *Olympus Tribune*. She sealed the envelope, pressing the flap firmly down with her fist. Then slowly she began to get ready.

Mechanically, she bathed and brushed her teeth and combed her hair. She pulled on her clothes, not thinking about anything at all. Somehow, she reflected, as she stood before her mirror and saw the image there, the anticipation she had had for this very moment had disappeared. Like a hill when you are riding toward it. She sighed a little as she found a ribbon for her hair. Opening her top drawer she fumbled around in its contents looking for a hair clip.

Maybe it was her imagination, she thought. She sniffed. She was sure she smelled the faint fragrance of a rose. She pulled the drawer out further, ruffling up its contents. There under her handkerchiefs was Mr. Harvey's rose. Ruthy picked it up, and the dried petals fell to the floor.

Her father was waiting at the bottom of the stairs. He stood there looking up at her as she came down.

"Well!" he said, pretending to be overcome at the sight. "Here comes the queen!"

Ruthy pulled up her gloves, and smoothed down her skirt, and said, "Oh, daddy."

"There's just one thing I want to know," he said when she came to the bottom step. His smile was quizzical. "You still thinking of changing Sunday schools?"

Startled, Ruthy looked at him. She hadn't thought about it, she reflected, not for a long time. She remembered the Sunday school party, and Mrs. Harrington. She heard again Mrs. Harrington's surprised voice — "*Sam* Morgen's daughter?"

Thoughtfully Ruthy said, "I couldn't even if I wanted to."

"Couldn't?" her father said, regarding her, his head to one side.

She hadn't fooled Mrs. Harrington one bit, she remembered. Ruthy answered her father's question.

"I guess it's because I'm Sam Morgen's daughter," she said. She smiled a little at her father's quick grin.

"Now about the cats — " he began, and stopped to clear his throat.

She said hurriedly, "Mrs. Byrd is keeping them for me tonight in her basement."

Mr. Morgen opened his eyes wide. "Mrs. Byrd?"

Ruthy smiled wryly. It was a pretty strange ending, she guessed, considering everything.

Her grandmother came hurrying in from the kitchen. She stopped as she saw Ruthy standing there, and she clasped her hands together with pride. Ruthy looked down at her feet.

"Like I said," her grandmother smiled and nodded, "it's a beginning. A Bas Mitzvah is always a beginning."

Her father said softly, "Like your grandmother said, it's a beginning."

Ruthy raised her head. He didn't mean her Bas Mitzvah. He meant Mrs. Byrd letting the cats sleep in her basement. Ruthy hadn't even thought of it that way. Suddenly she felt a prickling near the back of her neck. Her father meant endings could be beginnings just as the Rabbi had said.

"Are you ready?" her mother said coming in with her hat on.

Ruthy wriggled her shoulders. She looked at her father tying his tie and putting on his coat, and at her mother fixing the veil over her hat. She looked at her grandmother carefully buttoning up her neat black coat, and at her brother Herbert. She glanced over them, and then away, out the front window, down the street to where the small truck had gone.

"Of course," she almost shouted. "Of course!"